The Magicke Outhouse

Book Three of the Silverville Saga

Kym O'Connell-Todd
&
Mark Todd

Raspberry Creek Books, Ltd.

**RASPBERRY
CREEK**

BOOKS

The Magicke Outhouse

This book is a work of fiction. Names, characters, places, and incidents either are products of the authors' imaginations or are used fictitiously. Any resemblance to actual events or locales or persons, living or dead, is entirely coincidental.

ISBN 978-0-9851352-4-9
Library of Congress Control Number: 2013953527

Printed in the United States of America

www.raspberrycreekbooks.com

Raspberry Creek Books, Ltd.
Gunnison, CO   Tulsa, OK

Cover Design by
Kym O'Connell-Todd

Also by Kym O'Connell-Todd & Mark Todd

Little Greed Men:
Book One of the Silverville Saga
(Raspberry Creek Books)

All Plucked Up:
Book Two of the Silverville Saga
(Raspberry Creek Books)

The Magicke Outhouse:
Book Three of the Silverville Saga
(Raspberry Creek Books)

By Mark Todd

Strange Attractors:
A Story About Roswell
(Write in the Thick of Things)

Wire Song
(Conundrum Press)

Tamped, But Loose Enough to Breathe
(Ghost Road Press)

Acknowledgments

The authors wish to recognize several individuals who have contributed to the final version of this novel. We want to thank Alex J. Cavanaugh, Charlie Craig, and Stacia Deutsch – all authors whose work we admire and on whom we relied for thoughtful comments. A special thanks to Julie Leuk, T.L. Livermore, and Zac Thompson, who each agreed to read earlier drafts of the novel and offered insightful suggestions to strengthen the story's character development and overarching continuity. Thanks to pig wrangler and pig voice coach Marty Grantham for agreeing to let Breakfast be a character in this novel. And finally, warm thanks to Larry Meredith and the folks at Raspberry Creek Books, who make it possible for us to share the continuing stories of the Silverville Saga.

Kym dedicates this book to her parents,
Robert and Dee Johnson

Mark dedicates this book to his mother,
Mary K. Todd

The
Magicke
Outhouse

PROLOGUE

Massachusetts Bay Colony, 1662

An almost dreamlike voice, muffled and unintelligible, poked at the edges of his consciousness. As usual, the tones became words. In this case, dramatic and overbearing.

"They wring their hands, their caitiff-hands,
and gnash their teeth for terrour:
They cry, they roar, for anguish sore
and gnaw their tongues for horrour."

The pattern always started the same when he possessed a new body – drowsiness, disorientation and, finally, clarity.

The voice continued,

"But get away without delay,
Christ pities not your cry:
Depart to Hell, there may you yell,
and roar eternally."

Micah gazed around to see if he'd landed in the right place and the right time. Apparently so. All of the women in his line of vision wore long skirts, their faces hidden behind cotton bonnets knotted under the chin. The men, no less stiff-backed, wore dark-colored trousers above stockings of rust, brown, or green.

He looked down to discover his own clothing pretty much the same. Except that the buckles on his squared-toed shoes looked larger, shinier than those around him.

An elbow pushed hard against his frock waistcoat and he heard a whisper in his ear. "Thou hadst fallen asleep!"

Turning toward the whisper, he saw a pretty young woman meet his gaze, a slight frown crumpling her eyebrows. Fragile tendrils of copper hair escaped the hemmed edges of her bonnet. Long lashes framed eyes that matched the deepest blue skies he'd ever seen.

"Thou darest not risk the ire of the Reverend."

Micah barely heard what she said. Her lips were so pale, so pink, so perfect.

She turned away, like the rest of the congregation crammed into the wooden pews, giving full attention to the sour-faced fellow who grimaced as he waved a tightened fist from above the pulpit.

The preacher's voice boomed louder, and he glared directly at Micah and the young woman. "The Day of Doom is upon us, as Wigglesworth's poem predicts. We must remain vigilant in the Lord's war against the evil and wickedness amongst us."

Whatever. Micah's vigilance focused only on the babe sitting next to him, and he couldn't stifle a wide grin.

"Daniel!" the voice from the pulpit thundered, and the bony finger of the preacher pointed in his direction.

Everyone shifted to stare at Micah.

"Dost thou find this discourse amusing?"

The smile drained from his face and he looked to the young woman beside him for support, but she kept her head lowered. Clearly, everyone waited for him to respond.

"Sorry. I, uh, hasseleth you not," he stammered.

11

A pall of silence clamped over the congregation.

"'Hasseleth you'?" the preacher repeated. "What manner of speech is this?"

MICAH squinted against the sun's rays, which began to stretch across pastures to the east and into the commons area where he stood. Or sagged. The rough-hewn planks of the stocks chaffed his neck and both wrists. If he could have twisted far enough, he'd have seen the ribbon the town fathers had pinned to his frock shortly after the service on the previous day. The ribbon held the letter "I," which they told him signified "Indolence." Could have just as well stood for "Idiot." Maybe he should have kept his mouth shut, like he had on previous Day Trips.

Beside him lay a snoring man with ankles locked in foot stocks. Guess they only had one pair, which left the upright stocks for Micah. His back ached from a night half standing, half stooping, and he'd struggled to stay awake. Once he zonked, his stay in Puritan times would be over. But he wasn't ready to leave. Not just yet.

Signs of life stirred in the Puritan village. One man led a horse from a barn beside a two-story house. When Micah had first arrived, he'd expected to find wigwams and shanties, but this place was more like pictures he'd seen of quaint New England hamlets. Some of the homes around the commons had a combination of stone walls and parallel wooden slats. The windows even had glass. He watched a woman across the commons step outside one home and stuff loaves of bread into a Dutch oven. Within minutes, the smell wafted over the stocks, waking the man lying beside him. He had a big "D" on his ribbon. Micah figured it stood for "Drunkard," since he twisted on his side to puke out his guts.

Three little boys ran out from between two of the houses and headed straight toward Micah. They stopped short twenty feet away, hands behind their backs. After a sly nod, the tallest one pelted him first. Micah jerked his head to the side as much as the stocks would allow, but the semi-dry cow pie still hit him in the ear. The two younger boys hadn't perfected their aims, and their volleys struck Micah's shoes and one even exploded on the drunkard's chest.

At least the excitement jarred Micah more awake. "Wait 'til I'm out of here, you little shits!"

A female voice shouted from behind him, "Fie! Fie! Off with you, young ruffians."

The boys scattered and ran in different directions.

His pew partner – they'd called her Sarah – appeared with a pail of water and dipper in hand. She was still the knock-out he remembered from yesterday, but today's pinafore showed signs of morning chores. "Shhh! Daniel, thou must be more contrite. This is thy punishment for falling asleep in church and speaking rudely to my father."

"The preacher's your father?"

"The stocks have addled thy mind. Thou knowest my father has been minister of our parish all my sixteen years."

"Oh, right, I forgot...eth."

He'd hoped he would see her again before he had to leave. He felt a sudden pang of envy for Daniel and the obvious relationship between him and Sarah. Micah could barely talk to girls in his own time without stammering and turning red-faced.

She plunged the dipper into the pail and pressed it to his lips. "Thou needs must drink."

He slurped at the water, feeling it dribble down his chin. Sarah picked up the corner of her linen apron and dabbed at the droplets.

She glanced to either side, leaned close and whispered, "Perhaps a kiss from thy betrothed will better refresh thee."

He focused on her lips, moist and inviting.

13

But the kiss never came. He blinked and focused on the rubbery jowls of Buford Price.

CHAPTER ONE

"Wake up, boy!" Buford slapped Micah's cheeks. Damned kid. "You on drugs or something?"

Buford half pulled, half dragged Micah out of the old outhouse that sat on his newly acquired property. He kicked the door shut with his foot and propped the boy against the wooden siding. Micah shook his head like he was trying to shrug off a bad hangover, raising his hands to his face. Yeah, his cheeks must be smarting from the many times Buford had just slapped him.

"You scared the bejeezus out me, kid. I've been smacking you for fifteen minutes."

At that moment his helper for the day, Howard Beacon, ran over with a bucket of water, but tripped and spilled most of the contents all over his baggy pants and pigeon-toed feet before he could reach the outhouse. With a skinny arm, he offered the two inches of liquid left in the container.

Buford waved him off. "Never mind. Don't need it now."

Micah slid down to a squat. He still looked pretty dazed.

"What were you doing in my outhouse?" Buford demanded.

The boy said nothing.

My God, hope he doesn't need a doctor, Buford thought. He

didn't need a lawsuit right now. He'd just signed the papers to buy the place that morning. He couldn't afford to put out cash for litigation.

"Aren't you Micah Musil?"

The young man staggered to his feet and nodded his head. "Yeah."

Buford thought so. Broken home, single mom. And a reputation for being a recluse with his head always buried in books. Guess the poor kid had taken to drugs and alcohol, but Buford would be damned if it would happen on his property.

Within the next eight weeks, he planned to turn this wreck of an abandoned ranch into the finest shooting range that Silverville had ever seen. Those dilapidated barns – and outhouse – would be torn down and replaced with a back berm and targets. And the old garden transformed into a parking lot. After looking at several properties, Buford saw the potential of this location immediately. The isolation made sure no neighbors would complain about gunfire, and the price tag was hard to beat. First he'd sell the firearms and ammo at Price's Gun Paradise, the store he'd owned for fifteen years, and next he'd steer his clientele to Price's Shooting Paradise. But with a hefty membership fee for the privilege. Except for Alien Landing theme park, this might be the best scheme he'd thought up yet.

And a damned sight better than his failed ski resort. Wasn't his fault it never snowed enough to make a success out of Price's Ski Paradise. Pissed him off that everyone in town called it Buford's Folly instead. Well, no one would laugh at this venture. What could go wrong?

Then Buford scowled at Micah. This kid, and others like him, could make it go wrong.

"What if we'd flattened that outhouse while you were in it? Keep that in mind toward the end of the week when the bulldozer gets here." He pointed a finger at the driveway. "Get the hell out of here. If I see you trespassing again, I'm calling the cops." Buford turned to his helper. "Howard!"

The young man holding the near-empty water bucket jumped.

"Escort Micah off the property," Buford shouted.

Howard reached over and took Micah by the elbow and led him toward the driveway.

In the meantime, Buford shifted his attention to the project at hand. He marched to the largest barn and pulled open the door, stepping across old chicken wire and empty TV dinner trays. He might be able to salvage this building for an indoor shooting facility complete with moving targets. Why, he might even be able to attract the FBI for training exercises. He brushed a chicken feather from his shoulder and continued his assessment. Maybe those horse stall dividers could serve as concealments for the cardboard bad guys. And he could use those metal bars on the windows to construct some sort of tracking across the floor to fire at moving targets.

He walked back outside and headed to the old ranch house. He hadn't yet decided if he'd sic the bulldozer on this structure. The backdoor hung on one hinge and groaned as he pushed inside. The fumes of packrat droppings overwhelmed him even more than the first time he'd looked through the building, and he staggered back into the fresh air. A little remodeling, a broom, and some bleach might still salvage the place as a clubhouse. Even someone with half a brain, like Howard, could clean out all those turds.

"Uh, Mr. Price?"

There was the halfwit now, standing right behind him. "Howard, I have a really important job for you."

"Yeah, but I have something to tell you."

"Ride your bike back to town and get a broom." Buford extended his arm in a wide arc toward the ranch house. "I'm about to make you instrumental in this great business enterprise. I might even make you a partner – um, make that a junior partner."

Howard's eyes grew wide. "You will?"

"But you're gonna have to work hard. Behind every successful junior partner is the willingness to do stuff no one else wants to do."

"Oh boy, Mr. Price. I'll go get that broom right now." Howard turned and ran toward his bike.

Buford called after him, "Wait! You had something to tell me first?"

His new junior partner pushed his bicycle back to Buford. "Yes, I have something to tell you first."

Buford sighed. "Well, spit it out."

The junior partner levered his kickstand down and shuffled within inches of Buford's face.

"You know that outhouse we were just at?"

"Geez, Howard, just tell me!"

"It's where Micah time-travels."

MICAH tried to get his breathing under control as he walked home. His nagging cough didn't help.

How could he stop that asshole Buford Price from tearing down the outhouse? For several weeks, it had served as Micah's personal one-seater laboratory. The first time he took a "Day Trip" – at least, that's what he called them – it was a complete accident. He'd been out hiking early on a Saturday morning, thinking about the origins of alchemy in Ancient Egypt. He'd stopped to use the old outhouse. But when he stepped inside and sat down over the circular cutout in the bench, one that emitted peculiar fumes, he immediately found himself waking up in an Egyptian temple complex. He wandered down a hall where fresh paint adorned statues, and the mysterious glyphs looked new and gaudy. A few bald men wearing robes and sandals shuffled about a courtyard. One of them approached and appeared to scold him, but Micah had no idea what he said. He simply nodded and followed the man into a small dark room where a two-foot statue perched on a short stone pedestal. The man opened a chest and removed miniature garments and handed one of them to Micah. When his companion began to dress the statue, Micah did the same. So went the day – Micah following in the footsteps of his barking supervisor, trying to figure out what the guy wanted him to do. What a bossy prick. Once, when the priest left the room, Micah couldn't help himself. He raised his robe and watered the statue. They'd never know, what with all the incense and heavily scented oil they'd had him pour over the figure.

It was the longest and most realistic dream he'd ever had, and he wondered when he'd wake up. At the end of the day he collapsed, exhausted, on the pallet where he first found himself that morning.

In an instant, he discovered himself back in the outhouse, in the dark. And his watch told him twelve hours had passed. Had he hit his head on something that produced such an elaborate dream? What other explanation could there be? He raced home, but his mother didn't even notice he'd been gone.

The experience intrigued him, and the next weekend he returned with no great hope it would happen again. Just like before, his mind focused on alchemy, but this time not on its origins. Just in case this worked again, he didn't want to spend another day playing dolls with a statue. Instead, he thought about Medieval alchemists and their elaborate laboratories. He decided to replicate everything he'd done before: entering the outhouse, closing the door, and sitting on the one-holer. Once again, as the fumes hit his nostrils, the walls of the outhouse dissolved into a bare bedroom, furnished with a crude bedstead and table. Shelves along one wall held glass bottles with stoppers, mortars and pestles, and several rolled-up parchments. He slipped from the bed onto the stone floor and walked across the room to examine the equipment. After pulling the stoppers and sniffing the bottles, he recognized a few of the substances. Sulphur, mercury, and an odd assortment of compounds, including a fungus that smelled very similar to the acrid odor from the outhouse.

He was in an alchemist's laboratory! Maybe 15th or 16th Century, best he could tell.

Someone knocked at the door, and a woman entered carrying a tray of bread and cheese.

"Ihr Frühstück, mein Herr," she announced with diffidence.

Micah recognized her speech as German, and answered with one of the few words he knew. "Danke."

The woman retreated and closed the door behind her. Not wanting to repeat his moronic ignorance like he had in Egypt, Micah locked the door and spent the day puzzling over the apparatus, particularly the bottle of fungus.

And like his first Day Trip, when he at last lay down on the bed and closed his eyes, he returned to the outhouse.

Several more times during the next few weeks, he explored other dates and places where savants practiced alchemy. What he had come to discover was that his Day Trips always ended when he fell asleep. The couple of times he forced himself to stay awake, the trip ended anyway after about twenty-four hours, regardless of the situation. And he suspected the Day Trips had something to do with the fungus. He'd taken samples, but the experience still only occurred when inside that little privy.

He took longer strides on the road leading home as he thought about the potential of what he'd stumbled on. The outhouse was so much more than a *little privy*. It represented an extraordinary discovery, a window into the past like no one had ever experienced.

He remembered Buford's intention to "flatten" it. What a waste if that happened.

AS MICAH entered the tiny duplex where he lived with his mother, he found the house was empty, as usual. Dirty dishes filled the sink and the trashcan overflowed with two days' refuse. True, carrying out the trash fell to him as his part of the chores, but his mother had once again left the dishes in a pile – her contribution to the daily routine. The place wasn't really designed for two. His mother had the bedroom, and they'd propped a cheap accordion panel across the arch leading into the breakfast nook, which now served as his bedroom, complete with a bunk bed mattress pushed under the window on the floor to make room for a small table and folding chair. The table held his hand-me-down computer from his mom's boss. But with only dial-up Internet, it didn't much matter how old the desktop computer was.

He glanced with a little guilt at the ragged patch where a chunk of yellow plaster had dislodged off the wall beside the fridge – the aftermath of an argument a few nights ago he'd had with his mother's new boyfriend Glenn, the latest in a long string of losers she'd brought home. He wished he could've punched Glenn instead of the wall. When his mother mentioned the hole, he blamed faulty plaster, not his smoldering anger.

Micah opened the refrigerator door and looked behind a carton of outdated milk. He grabbed the bread bag, pulled out two slices, and carried them around the kitchenette to decide what to put between them. All he found in the cupboard was a small tin of Vienna sausages. Those and three or four aspirin would have to be dinner tonight.

Shoving aside the accordion panel with his hip, he dropped into the folding chair and turned on the computer.

While he waited for the old machine to boot up and dial in, he munched on the sandwich. He glanced at the night class books piled beside the computer and groaned. His mother came up with the idea of night classes, not him, when he washed out halfway through the first semester at college. She insisted he continue his studies somehow or other. And he had, but on his own terms. It just didn't include formal schooling. He hated those general education classes, where the professors told him what to learn and how to digest it. And it bugged him that he had to take Chem 101 when he'd already been showing his junior high school science teachers the correct way to represent specific isotopes in nuclear equations. For some reason, his interest in alchemy and how it shaped the future of chemistry pissed off his college teacher, eventually leading to his suspension. So he decided to study it on his own.

He looked at the clock on the wall. 6:30 p.m. His mother wouldn't be home from her job at the Last Call Bar for six more hours.

The computer still struggled to boot up. He unplugged it from the wall, opened a few textbooks to make it look like he'd been studying, and headed out the door to the library, where the Internet connection was faster.

Tomorrow morning, he'd pay a visit to Buford Price.

APRIL bounded down the sidewalk, crossed the street, and turned to face the steps leading inside an impressive, century-old, two-story red stone building. Its steep-pitched rooflines with transepting gables reminded her of an old church. The high wall of the façade surrounding the main entrance reached the entire height of the street-side gable, the top edges stair-stepping to a point.

The library.

She paused before entering to take in its allure. She'd loved libraries since her early childhood in Suffolk, England, where her father served two years as a jet mechanic. Hot summers had driven her inside, the cool walls insulating the base's children from sultry temperatures. The smell of books intoxicated her as much as the cool air. Every time the Air Force moved her family, the local library became a favorite haunt. Books fascinated her, particularly those about history.

She climbed the stairs and opened the heavy door of the Silverville Public Library.

An older woman standing behind the circulation desk looked up. Had to be Miss Brumbelow, head librarian. The woman smiled and said, "Can I help you with anything?"

April marched to the desk and thrust out her hand. "I'm April."

The smile melted into a frown. "Your internship started yesterday."

"Didn't you get my message?" *The one I never sent.*

"No, I don't recall any messages from you."

April forced a cough and drew a tissue from her pocket. "Really? You didn't get my note about my recent relapse?"

Miss B appeared to wait for more of an explanation, which April was happy to provide.

"The Uruguayan Flying Worm Syndrome. It flared up again."

"Excuse me? Uruguay? I understood you came from Placer City."

"That's where I grew up, after a traveling circus brought me into the United States and my parents adopted me." April blew her nose long and hard into the tissue. "I caught the worm before that, when I was only six. Most people die from it. I was lucky."

The librarian's eyes narrowed. "Is it contagious?"

"Not once the worms work their way out of your system. Mine have." April offered a long-suffering shrug. "But once you get it, it stays with you the rest of your life."

"Is that why your pupils are so … so pink?"

April bent her head and plucked a small disk from one eye and held it up on her finger for the woman to inspect. "Lavender."

"Excuse me?

"Colored contacts. They're lavender."

While April replaced the theatrical lens, Miss B heaved a

disappointed sigh and retrieved a sheet of paper from under the desk. "Here are the responsibilities I've typed up for you." She handed it to her new intern and motioned for her to follow.

April watched Miss B's broad backside waddle down an aisle pushing a cart laden with books ready to re-shelve. Maybe she'd laid it on a bit thick with the circus story. Miss B didn't appear to buy it. But the tale just sprang out of her mouth before she had a chance to think it through. All her life she'd re-invented herself at each new base as a way to impress strangers and make new friends. It came so naturally to her. Even now, after three years of college and into her first internship for her library science major.

Several years ago, her parents had taken her to a counselor to address her overactive imagination. He'd told them many intelligent kids – and after all, she *was* intelligent, having skipped a couple grades – often supplemented their reality, particularly those continuously uprooted because of the transient nature of military life. He told them not to worry, she'd outgrow it. But she hadn't yet nor did she want to. She enjoyed twisting reality for her audience, and of course they understood it was just a performance. Well, usually.

The librarian droned on about call letters and filing protocols as she slotted books onto the rows of shelves. "We use the Dewey Decimal instead of Library of Congress classification system because patrons find it easier to use and..."

April understood both systems already and tuned her out, more interested in the chance to look at the local history section. After her dad retired and they moved to Placer City, just an hour away, she'd spent her senior year in high school hearing all the stories about Silverville. UFOs, curses, ley lines. Placer City never had that much excitement – well, except for the unsolved murder on the pass halfway between the two towns a few years back. She was eager to dive into library holdings on the local phenomena.

"...What do you think, Miss Schauers?" the librarian asked.

April had been nodding her head at the background noise of Miss B's voice, but she had no idea what the conversation entailed. "I think there's somebody over there who needs my help."

She dashed over to an older man with wavy white hair sitting cross-legged on the floor facing a shelf of books. He did a double-take when he looked up into her lavender pupils and politely turned away.

"Are you finding what you're looking for?" she asked.

The selections he perused sported titles like *Piracy on the Open Seas*, *Plunder and Booty,* and *An Index to Ancient Topographical Maps*. "Just getting ideas for my next vacation."

"Or researching locations for buried treasure?" She laughed at her own clever response, but he didn't. Maybe her little joke hit where X marked the spot.

"Could be," he answered.

She squatted next to him. "I'm April, the new library intern." She bent closer to his ear and in a lower voice added, "Please let me help you. I'm trying to impress my supervisor, Miss B – er, Brumbelow."

He considered her for a moment, and then said in a voice a bit too loud for the library, "Why yes, I *could* use some help."

Miss B, who'd been staring at April, turned and pushed her book cart away.

"Thanks!" she whispered. "You know, first day and all. I really can help you, Mr....?"

"Call me Perry." He reached out and shook her hand. "Retired and bored out of my mind. I'm looking for a new adventure."

"If you're interested in pirate treasure, you should check out the coasts of Madagascar. My parents are ocean archaeologists and –"

"—I know that area," Perry interrupted. "I led an expedition down there some years back. We found a sunken Roman galley filled with artifacts. Unfortunately, I hadn't cleared the excavation with the proper authorities, and they confiscated everything, threw me in jail, and I had a devil of a time convincing them I wasn't a looter." He gave her a knowing wink.

I can top that, April thought. But at that moment, Miss B's cart rounded the corner and approached.

"Glad to help." April stood. "If there's anything else you need, let me know."

And so went her day, assisting people, giving them valuable advice and tidbits that might have been true. Or not.

By late afternoon, April sought out Miss B to find out when her shift would end.

"Not until 7 p.m.," the librarian told her. "Or whenever the last patron leaves."

April forced another cough.

"If your worms will permit." Miss Brumbelow spun on her heels and walked away.

In an attempt to look busy, April headed for the paranormal section and pretended to straighten and reorder books. Yes, here was one on ley lines, those mysterious magnetic fields that supposedly crisscrossed the Earth. She'd heard when they intersected one another, strange things happened.

Behind her, sitting at a computer terminal was a young man about her age, swearing under his breath. She walked over to the table, still holding her open book, and sat down beside him to offer her assistance.

He turned his head and glanced at her book. "That's it."

"Excuse me?"

"The one I'm looking for."

Even sitting down, the young man was tall, had to be well over six feet. His hair looked like ripe prairie grass swept up by the wind and in need of mowing. She handed over the book, which he took eagerly and bent to read. April mimicked his forward bend and tilted her head to see his face. Did he wear theatrical contacts as well? His eyes almost looked too pale blue for natural coloring. Kind of cute.

"Are you interested in ley lines, too?" she asked. She saw his eyes flick in her direction without moving his head and return to the book.

"Um, yeah."

"Me, too. Why are you interested?"

Micah wished she'd go away.

"Well, why are you interested?" she asked.

Before he could respond, she continued, "I'm April, by the way, the new library intern. My real name is Nadya. My real parents were Soviet KGB double agents, but they were shot and killed. My new parents traveled to a Gulag in Russia and adopted me when I was only six. But you better call me April."

Micah tried to ignore her and started reading a passage out of the ley line book:

> There are specific sites on the planet allegedly filled with mystical energy – i.e., Stonehenge, Mount Everest, Ayers Rock, Nazca, the Great Pyramid, and Sedona. Advocates claim that this mystical energy is connected to variations of magnetic fields. Maps have been created to record the locations of intersecting ley lines (see appended map at end of book).

He flipped to the inside cover and opened the fold-out map. There, right over Silverville, six lines intersected. To his dismay, April flattened the map and turned it in her direction.

She tapped her finger about where Silverville should be. "Holy Cow! I bet that explains all the weird shit that happens around here."

And possibly responsible for my Day Trips, Micah thought. He suspected a combination of phenomena once his fungus samples failed to work alone. He tugged the map back into view. Sure, lots of other things had occurred around the town, but the outhouse had to sit at Ground Zero of the ley line intersections.

He needed to have a better idea – more ammunition – to explain how the Day Trips worked before he approached Mr. Price.

Still staring at the map, he asked, "What do you have on Ancient Egypt?"

"Why don't you ever look at me when you talk?"

With a reluctant shift, Micah turned to face her. April/Nadya wasn't at all what he expected in a librarian. Black hair, bobbed in a 1920s style, sat atop a cute girl with a petite figure dressed in a sequined sweater and pink poodle skirt that matched the color of her eyes. Wait a minute, lavender eyes?

She caught his stare and plucked out a lens. "Different color for each day of the week."

He cleared his throat and looked away. "Oh, sure."

"You wearing them, too?" She replaced the lens. "I mean, your eyes are an odd color. Pretty, but odd."

Micah snapped his book shut, stood, and started to leave.

She jumped up and stayed in step with him. "Didn't you want a book on Ancient Egypt? I don't know what the library has, but give me a sec to look."

He hesitated. He did need more information.

April must have taken his pause as a sign, and said. "Wait right here."

She marched off, her saddle shoes clopping against the hard wooden floor. He walked back to the table and reopened the ley line book.

Minutes later, he heard her shoes stop behind his chair.

"Okay, I've got one," she announced.

He held out his hand without turning around.

"Uh, uh. Not 'til you tell me your name, and what you're researching."

Micah swiveled in the chair to see her standing with her arms behind her back, waiting.

"Aren't you closing pretty soon?" Micah asked.

"Yep, so you better hurry up and tell me."

"I'm looking for –"

"Nope. Name first."

He sighed. "Micah."

April sat down and dropped the book on the table, keeping her hand flat and firm on the cover. "And?"

"And I'm not really sure, maybe something about the how Egyptians separated out the soul. I think I read about that once."

With her free hand, she grabbed the chair's wooden arm, bumping and scooting it closer to him. "I can tell you all about that. They broke it into the Ka and the Ba and the Akh."

"Oh yeah, I sort of remember something about that."

She talked right over him. "The Ka is the life force and needed a body that had to be fed. The Ba is the personality. It could leave the tomb and go all over the place. When a person died, the life force and personality joined the Akh."

Considering her outlandish Russian tale, he wondered if she was making up some of these details, too. It must have showed. "You don't believe me?" She opened the book to the table of

29

contents, found what she was looking for, and pointed to a page. She shoved the book into his hands. "Here, 289."

Micah skimmed for a couple of minutes. There, displayed in print, just as she'd said. April/Nadya at least told the truth about this.

CHAPTER TWO

"So you think you can have the bulldozer here day after tomorrow?" Buford asked into his cell. Besides a hot-air balloon touring service, Bob Hardin operated the only for-hire dozer in Silverville. Buford wanted it here yesterday – the day he signed the papers – but he'd have to take what he could get. "Just a couple of sheds and an outhouse. Shouldn't take you more than half a day."

He backed out of the building as Howard swept the floor. The old ranch house would take a lot more than half a day to make it into the clubhouse he envisioned.

"Another thing," he continued, "I need you to build a berm behind the shooting targets. So maybe a whole day, tops."

He snapped the phone shut, satisfied Bob could meet his deadline. He peered in the window to check Howard's progress. Buford's junior partner had gathered all the debris in the living room to one side and finished sweeping the floor. Now he was moving the debris to the opposite side to sweep the other half.

Buford tapped on the pane and shouted, "Just pick that stuff up and cart it out before you start the other side."

Howard approached the window from inside. He pulled down the bandana covering his mouth and pointed back to the jumble of rat droppings, dried leaves, and torn tiling. "You mean this stuff?" "And when you're through, make sure you –." The phone rang again, interrupting Buford's instructions. It was the contractor, explaining he couldn't get over to the site for a couple of weeks.

"Now hold on just a minute. Didn't I just sell you that high-powered rifle at cost?" *Well, mostly at cost.* "I was hoping you'd return me the favor and get your butt out here in the next few days."

At that moment, Howard backed out the door, balancing an armful of dust and tiles that mostly trailed behind him.

"Hold on a sec." Buford covered the mouthpiece. "Geez, Howard, get the goddam wheelbarrow!" *A wonder that boy has made it his whole thirty years.*

For the next several minutes, the phone conversation consisted of bargaining and cajoling on both sides.

"I want a cocktail bar all along the inside east wall," Buford explained. He listened to the contractor for a few minutes, absently looking through the door at the collapsed ceiling in the kitchen, the ragged hole in the dining room wall, the torn-up linoleum throughout. "Naw, it'll just take a few nails and a can of paint. Why don't you just give me a bid over the phone?"

A crash reverberated across the yard, and Howard yelped. Half the barn's double door lay shattered on top of the wheelbarrow, the young man struggling to hold up the remaining half before it fell, too.

"Gotta run. Call you later." Buford pocketed his phone and shuffled toward the barn as quick as his fat, short legs would take him. But he didn't move fast enough. Just as he raised his hands to help support the semi-prone door looming over Howard, the younger man's strength gave out, and the weight pushed both of

32

them to their knees and then onto their backs, the door pressing down on top.

"For Pete's sake," Buford said, shouting into the wood that pinned his head to the ground. "What happened here?"

"The barn door fell on us."

Spitting a splinter from his lip, Buford lamented, "Master of the obvious, as always."

He heard a scuffing of gravel beyond the heavy door, and he turned his head to squint at a man's feet at eye level. "Get us outta here!"

The feet moved away and crunched to the other end of the door. The feet's owner said, "Do I hear voices?"

"Micah, goddammit, is that you? Get us out of here!"

"Yes, I do believe I hear voices."

The feet returned once again, replaced by a head filling Buford's narrow sight of the outside world.

"What are you guys doing under there? Male bonding?"

The barn door began to rise from one end, enough for the two men to squirm out.

"GOOD God, Micah, you showed up in the nick of time," Buford wheezed, staggering over to a couple of weathered hay bales.

He chose the cleanest one and plopped his backside down. Micah and Howard shared the other bale.

"Hey," Buford said, "what are you doing here? I thought I kicked you off the place."

The boy stared at the backpack in his lap and nodded. "Good thing I did come by, or you'd still be trapped under that door."

"We had it under control," Buford blustered.

"Yeah, right. You need to hear what I have to say before you tear that outhouse down."

33

"Howard already told me about that time-travel stuff. You should ease up on whatever drugs you're smoking."

"It's not drugs. This really happens, and the outhouse has something to do with it."

Buford doubled over with a belly laugh. "You mean it's a *magic* outhouse?" Amused at his oxymoron, he began another fit of cackling.

Neither Micah nor Howard joined him.

"I know it's hard to believe, but listen to this," Micah said.

Somewhere in his head, Buford could hear Micah explaining the connection the kid thought existed between the outhouse and the fungus inside. But Buford had more pressing issues. He hadn't decided yet what sort of a sign he should erect on the road. Of course, it would announce Price's Shooting Paradise, maybe in blinking lights. And he needed a catchy slogan.

"Only the combination of the fungus and the outhouse allows me to take my Day Trips – well, that's what I call them."

That kid's gotta go, Buford thought. So many details to hash out. He'd want to print up flyers to place in the gun shop, and he needed to work out the deals for membership in the shooting club.

Out of the corner of his eye, he saw Micah reach into his bag and withdraw a book. The boy opened it and started to explain about the strange phenomena created by magnetic fields and ley lines. Then he unfolded a map. "See how the lines intersect right over Silverville? And where the outhouse sits must be Ground Zero."

The lines converging on Silverville reminded Buford just how well situated the town was located in the middle of the country. Maybe he could buy billboards on some of the roads leading into the state. If only he could think, but that boy kept droning on.

34

"The fungus growing in there is something ancient alchemists believed was significant. It's got to somehow play into the time travel. But I can tell you it doesn't work by itself – I've tried it."

Buford pulled a handkerchief from his pocket, blew mightily, and then examined the contents.

Micah continued, "A couple of other things I've discovered. When you're inside, you'll go to whatever time-frame you're thinking of."

Buford stuffed the hanky back in his pocket. "I s'pose you're an expert on this now."

"I've done it a half dozen times. And each time, I could only go back and stay there for about twenty-four hours, or until I fell asleep."

"Yeah, well, Howard has to get back to work, and I've got more phone calls to make."

"There's more. It's not the kind of time-travel you're probably thinking …"

Without letting him finish, Buford ordered Howard to again escort Micah from the property.

"To knock that outhouse down would be like killing Bigfoot and burning his body," Micah shouted back as he and Howard walked down the driveway. "You'll be destroying a portal, something science has never seen before!"

Buford flipped open his cellphone and dialed the lumber yard. As he waited for someone to answer, he heard Micah's fading voice.

"Besides, who wouldn't want to time-travel?"

BUFORD tossed and turned, twisting his blankets into a corkscrew. He couldn't sleep. Too many details to work out with the upcoming new venture. Remodeling, contractors, lumber supplies – the list went on and on.

He looked at the alarm clock – four-thirty. Might as well get out of bed; he'd been awake the past two hours anyway, ever since he'd gotten up to pee. Damned prostate. He ought to be more conscientious about taking those pills the doctor had prescribed. Throwing off the covers, he moseyed into the kitchen to brew a pot of coffee.

He retrieved the weekly newspaper from his porch stoop, still lying there from yesterday. While the coffee dripped, he slouched into a chair and opened the *Silverville Valley Telegraph*. On the front page, the headlines proclaimed, "Local man wins state lotto." The picture showed the smiling winner, holding a giant check for two and half million bucks. Buford's stomach lurched. It was that son-of-a-bitch Earl Bob Jackson – mayor and wife-stealer. Just a few years ago, Skippy had been *his* wife until Jackson came to town, wooing all the women with his charm and his government UFO investigator badge. The worst part was that Buford had been the one to invite him to town after Howard had seen his flying saucer.

If Buford had owned a dog, he'd have kicked it.

Screw the coffee. He opened the top door of the liquor cabinet and splashed three fingers of bourbon into a glass and swilled it down in a single gulp. Then he slammed the glass at the wall. It didn't break. He ran into the bedroom, pulled on one shoe, and returned to stomp the glass into tiny shards. Next, he marched, sock and shoe, over to the kitchen table and ripped off the front page of the newspaper and crumpled it. Holding it over the sink, he reached for a kitchen match and set the offending photo ablaze. When the fire approached his fingers, he dropped it, the edges hissing against water droplets in the porcelain basin.

"Burn, you bastard!"

Buford would have hated anybody local who'd won the lotto, but Earl Bob Jackson was a double insult. He could almost see that son-of-a-bitch wasting his newfound wealth on heart-bleeding charities or community playground equipment. *Need a new swing set? No problem. Need a new wing to the library? My pleasure.*

Buford would never squander money on worthless entitlement projects. No siree, a much bigger community favor would be to expand the shooting range, making marksmanship available to all. He plopped down on a kitchen chair, belching sour bourbon. So much good he could have done with those millions. If only *he* had won the lottery. If he could only turn back the clock and buy that tic –"

Who wouldn't want to time-travel?

He would, of course, to the day before the lotto drawing. His body tensed with an involuntary intake of breath. Scrambling to his feet, he lurched to the sink, snatching up the still smoking newspaper page. He batted at the singed, fire-brittled article. Most of it had been destroyed, but there they were, still visible – the winning lottery numbers. Finally exhaling with relief, he tore off the remaining section with the numbers and clenched the scrap in his hand.

While he dressed, Buford considered what he was about to do. He must be crazy. Still, no one would witness his unlikely success at – what had that nerdy kid called it? – his "Day Trip." The bulldozer wouldn't show up until tomorrow, and Howard had to work at the funeral home most of the day.

What a long shot. Micah was surely on drugs. Yet, strange things did happen in Silverville. And Buford would try anything to thwart Earl Bob from winning that ticket.

He walked to his car and climbed in. What had Micah said about the how the outhouse worked?

BUFORD studied the structure before him – dilapidated, weathered, hardly worth saving. What was he thinking? This could never work. But if it did, he'd be the winner of the lotto prize and, more important, Earl Bob would not. He patted his pants to make sure the number was still in his pocket, took a deep breath, and opened the door of the old privy.

That's when the smell hit him. Methane and decomposing waste. But there was another odor, too – mossy, vegetative – possibly the fungus Micah had rattled on about.

With a furtive glance around him to make sure he remained alone, Buford stepped in and shut the door. Little light penetrated the small enclosure except through the vertical cracks in the time-shrunken slats. Buford could make out a bench with a covered hole. What he didn't see was the rusty nail for toilet paper, which immediately snagged his pants, leaving a small tear.

Settling on the bench against one wall, he fingered the new rip in his khakis and tried to recall what Micah had said. Something about just thinking where and what time-frame you wanted to go. He concentrated on the lottery drawing date the week before, and in Silverville, of course.

Five minutes later, he still sat there and nothing had happened.

Well, this is a royal waste of time. What was he missing? What else had Micah told him? Buford slapped his hand down on the covering to the one-holer in frustration. Did the kid say you needed to sit on it? Just to be on the safe side, he pulled up the cover, gagging at the fumes. Not sure what the next step should be, Buford pulled down his pants and repositioned himself over the opening.

ONCE upon a time there was a Queen who had a beautiful baby daughter," April began. She looked around at her audience of a dozen pre-schoolers, mothers, and one familiar-looking skinny guy who had to be pushing thirty. He was the only one really paying attention.

Okaaaay.

Mrs. B had suggested April take over library story time on her second day because she was "so good at making things up." April eagerly accepted the duty. Better than shelving books or culling the stacks, which had occupied the entire morning. After lunch, she'd spent a half hour skimming fairy tales, looking for just the right story – one she could make more interesting.

She looked back down at the story book and read. "The Queen asked all the fairies in the kingdom to the christening, but unfortunately forgot to invite one of them, who was a bit of a witch as well. She came anyway, but as she passed the baby's cradle, she said, 'When you are sixteen, you will injure yourself with a spindle and die!'"

A few minutes into the story, most of the kids had already drifted asleep; one focused on blowing bubbles with his spit. The mothers huddled, whispering and giggling at some private joke. The only person listening was the skinny guy, who sat cross-legged in rapt attention.

She beefed up the volume. "'Oh, no!' screamed the Queen in horror. A good fairy told the Queen not to worry because the girl would fall into a very deep sleep instead of dying. The fairy chanted a good magic spell.'"

The skinny guy raised his hand.

She paused but he continued to hold up his hand, saying nothing.

"Yes?"

The skinny guy lowered his hand and said, "We have a magic outhouse that puts people to sleep."

April waited for the punch line. He didn't seem to have one.

Time to improvise. "A magic outhouse, huh? Just so happens this story has a magic outhouse, too. So one day the Queen followed a frog into the Magic Outhouse where he gave her some special beans. She took them home and planted them. They soon turned into a big stalk that grew all the way into the clouds. The

Queen climbed it, and on top she found a handsome prince with long golden hair. 'Peace, baby,' he told her. They climbed down. The prince kissed the princess, and they all moved to Haight-Ashbury, where they lived happily ever after. The End."

By this time, not a single kid remained awake. The mothers looked up, clearly disappointed the story had already ended. Grumbling, they gathered their sleeping babes and filed out of the library.

Only the young man stayed behind. "That's not how the magic outhouse works."

"And your name is?"

"Howard. Howard Beacon."

April flipped through her mental files. "Hey, you're quite the celebrity." The guy who'd seen the aliens. "I thought I recognized you from the newspaper articles."

Howard nodded. "No beans in our outhouse, but you do fall asleep inside."

"Uh-huh." *Delusional? Maybe what happens when you live in Silverville too long.* She excused herself to straighten the chairs where the mothers had sat.

"Then you time-travel. That's what Micah says he does."

April spun to look at him. "Micah? Tall guy, sandy-colored hair?"

"Yep."

Couldn't be the same guy. When he was in there the previous night, he appeared normal enough. Even by her standards, a time-traveling outhouse seemed like a pretty tall tale. Wait a minute – this was bullshit. Time travel? In an outhouse? What a jerk to feed such a line to this poor challenged man. "Don't believe everything Micah says."

"Micah's my friend. He wouldn't lie." He shook her hand with vigor. "Thank you for the story time." He stared at her for a moment like it was her turn to say something.

Fairytale's over, fella. April smiled sympathetically and gestured toward the front door.

"Well, I gotta go work now," he said. "See you next week."

The odd little man walked out of the library, leaving April fuming at how Micah had purposely made a fool out of him.

"JUNIOR, I told you to get your butt out of bed!"

An acrid aroma of ammonia replaced the methane and fungal fumes of the instant before. Buford leaped out of the bed and looked down at abnormally small feet below flannel pajamas covered with cowboys and lariats.

The door swung open and an angry-looking woman glared at him. "You better not have wet that bed again, young man."

A small yellow circle stained the sheets where his butt had been.

"Off with those pants, mister!" The woman didn't wait for his response but pushed him onto the bed and yanked off the pajama bottoms.

"What the hell!" Buford exclaimed.

She smacked him across the mouth. "Wait 'til I tell your father what you just said. Now get changed and come downstairs before you're late for school."

She stormed out of the room, leaving Buford open-mouthed and bare-butted.

Stunned, he surveyed the small bedroom, trying to make sense out of what just happened. An assortment of model airplanes cluttered the dresser top, a baseball bat and glove leaned against a corner, posters of celebrity athletes plastered one whole wall.

How could he get back to the outhouse? He clenched his eyes shut and tried to transport himself to the building site of Price's Shooting Paradise. But when he looked again, the same disheveled room still lay sprawled around him.

41

"Junior, if you don't get down here, I'm coming up to smack you again!" the woman hollered from somewhere in the house.

He shoved through a pile of clothes on the floor, desperate to find his khakis with the lottery number in the pocket. All he found was a little pair of jeans and a striped shirt in sizes he hadn't been able to fit into for thirty years. In the closet, he sorted through shoes, trying to match a pair of sneakers.

All dressed, he poked his head out the bedroom door, almost colliding with the angry woman. She grabbed him by the collar and pulled him down the stairs.

Buford whined, "I'm sick."

"Not as sick as you're gonna be if you don't get on that bus. It's already here."

She shoved him out the front door and watched as he walked to the school bus waiting at the curb. With no chance for escape, Buford climbed the steps into the vehicle and took a seat among the clamoring children. Once the bus got underway, he felt a series of wraps on the back of his head and twisted to locate the source.

A freckly little snot sneered at him. "Hey, butthead, what took you so long? Kissing your *mommy* good-bye?"

All the other kids started laughing.

This can't be happening. He was a fortysomething-year-old man, divorced, a successful entrepreneur, a respected member of the community. Not a three-and-half-foot-tall brat. How would he get to the convenience store to buy the winning ticket if he was stuck in school all day? He'd escape, that seemed the only plan of action that made sense.

The numbers for the ticket! They were in Buford's pocket, not this kid's. Out of reflex, he jammed his hands into the little jeans – completely empty except for a smooth rock and a half-eaten candy bar.

Damn that Micah. This was *not* how he'd explained the time travel – or had he? Buford recalled Micah's admonition that the experience would not be what he would expect. But the Day Trips only lasted for twenty-four hours, he did remember Micah saying that. Or until he fell asleep first. That would give him time to salvage this trip.

As the bus motored along, he began to recognize hometown landmarks. At least he was in Silverville, but he didn't know if the outhouse had deposited him on the right day – it sure hadn't given him the right body.

"Hey, anybody know what day it is?" he shouted to no one in particular.

A barrage of chewed gum and paper spit wads pelted him from all directions.

A voice behind him yelled, "A school day, you dumb-ass!"

This approach got him nowhere. He decided to keep a lower profile for the rest of the trip to school, and he stared out the window. They traveled past the bank marquee, showing the date and time. A wave of relief washed over his tiny, sweaty body. Correct day. The numbers would be drawn that night. Good thing he'd memorized them. Well, mostly.

Turning onto Main Street, the bus stopped at the first light. Buford pressed his nose against glass at the sight of Price's Gun Paradise. In the store front window, he saw the partially built displays he had set up just a week before. A man struggled to drag a taxidermied carcass onto a stand next to the curb. The figure looked familiar somehow...

"That's me out there!"

More laughter. The kid sitting next to him on the seat groaned. "You wanna be him? That old fat guy, Buford Price? Everybody knows what an asshole he is."

Buford's mouth fell open. "Who says?"

"My dad."

Buford puffed up his little-boy chest. "What's your name, boy?"

43

"Oooh, I'm the Boogey Man." The child held up his hands and wiggled his fingers.

Deflated, Buford slumped against the bench seat and remained silent for the rest of the ride.

When the bus arrived at Silverville Elementary School, the gang of kids stormed out of the vehicle and toward the building. Buford pushed against the flow and tried to dodge away to make good an escape.

"Where you going, Junior?" A tall man with an orange vest grasped him behind the neck and pushed him all the way inside, down a hallway, and through a classroom door.

Only one empty desk remained. Buford trudged over and sat down. Moments later, a stout woman strutted through a side door and to a large square desk at the front of the room. *Oh my God, it's Mrs. Blutkopf.* Buford's fourth-grade teacher. He couldn't believe she was still teaching. Damn, now that he looked around, he realized it was the same room, too. Now it really felt like a time warp.

He spent the morning pretending to do lessons in social studies while trying to think of a way to skip out and get to the convenience store. He also had to figure out a way to find some money to buy the ticket. He thought he'd come up with a good plan, but when he got caught trying to steal money out of Mrs. Blutkopf's purse during recess, he realized it wasn't such a good plan after all.

"Junior! What are you doing!"

The old lady dragged him by the ear to the principal's office, where he was to spend the next hour writing the words "I will not steal" on a blank tablet. After the seventy-ninth time, he raised his hand and asked to go to the bathroom.

For once, he was glad of his diminutive size. The window in the bathroom would just let him squeeze through.

BUFORD wandered down an aisle in the convenience store, trying to figure out how he could hustle the two bucks for the ticket out of some poor sucker in the store.

He couldn't believe his good luck. In walked Howard Beacon.

Running up to the man, Buford blurted, "Hi, Howard."

"Hi, Junior. What are you doing here?"

"I'm supposed to buy some milk for my sick sister, but I lost my money."

Howard scratched his head. "When did you get a sister?"

Regroup. "I mean, my cousin. Can you loan me two dollars?"

Reaching into his pocket, Howard pulled out a billfold and handed him the two bills.

"Thanks!" Without waiting for a reply, Buford threaded his way around the shelves to the counter. He plopped the money down and asked for a lotto ticket.

"Not a quick pick. I've got my own numbers."

The man behind the counter shook his head and slid the dollars back at him. "Sorry, kid. You gotta be eighteen to buy or redeem a ticket."

Buford took the money and stepped back. There had to be a way around this. He looked at Howard, who stood at the other end of the store holding a bag of potato chips in each hand, hefting them as though trying to decide which identical bag he wanted. Buford stuffed the money in his jeans and walked over to him.

"I just remembered," Buford said. "Last night I saw aliens. Maybe the same ones you saw."

Howard nodded knowingly.

"They said they had a message for you," Buford continued.

"Another one?"

Howard had always claimed aliens had given him a message when he saw lights in the forest several years ago. Fortunately, he could never remember what it was, and Buford had happily planted alternative messages for whatever the situation had dictated.

"They sure did. They said, 'Howard Beacon is going to buy the winning lotto ticket.' And they gave me the numbers."

"They did?"

Poor dumb schmuck. He won't even know what to do with the money. Buford, of course, would help him with that – that is, when he could ditch this kid's body. With just a few hours left, he should get back to the outhouse in plenty of time before Howard cashed his check.

MICAH was staring into his face.

"Wake up, Mr. Price. You've just been on a Day Trip."

And thank God I had return passage. Buford yanked up his pants, marveling and relieved that they were once again size 44. He zipped up and staggered as he stepped out the door and pulled free as Micah tried to steady him at the elbow.

"By God, boy, you were right."

"Where did you go?"

To hell and back. "I was a damned little kid! You didn't tell me that could happen."

"You didn't give me a chance." Micah followed a step behind. "I tried to tell you it might not be what you expected."

Buford stomped toward his car but then stopped and burst into laughter. He'd left Junior in a heap of trouble.

Micah caught up. "It's just your consciousness – or your Ba – not your body, that makes the Day Trip. Seems to land in the first sleeping person it finds. There's no guarantee who that might be."

"I don't know what the hell you're talking about, but meet me at the Lazy S in thirty minutes, and we'll discuss this more."

Buford climbed into his silver Audi sedan and gunned the engine. As he turned onto the highway back to town, he smiled at his cleverness. By now, Howard had won the lotto and would need guidance on where to spend all that cash. Buford had lots of ideas, mostly involving Price's Shooting Paradise. Two and a half million bucks would go a long ways into renovating that old ranch house.

He drove past Alien Landing on the outskirts of town, nearly running down a family heading across the pavement to the theme park.

Screw renovating. He'd pull down the structure and build a brand new clubhouse, complete with swimming pool and high hedges all around the complex to protect the privacy of his exclusive clientele. Course, he'd be fair to Howard and offer him a full partnership – but it shouldn't get in the way of his regular duties of sweeping floors and cleaning toilets.

Money would never be a problem again. If he ran short, he'd simply make a new Day Trip to cash in on another lotto drawing. He might even diversify and start a chain of gun stores and shooting ranges. Hell, he might even play the stock market since he'd have some insider information. Just go back a few years, invest cheap, and come back a wealthy man.

He'd found the proverbial golden egg and the goose to keeping laying it whenever he wanted. Bob wouldn't be bulldozing that outhouse. Micah was right about saving it after all. *Oh yeah... Micah.* What if the kid wanted in on this? Buford didn't need another partner. All he needed from Micah was a few more details. Then he'd build a tall electrified perimeter fence to prevent anyone else from using what belonged to him.

Pulling into his driveway, Buford parked the Audi and lumbered toward the house. Just as he'd hoped, the weekly paper still lay bundled on the stoop beside his front door. He already knew the altered page-one story but relished the thought of opening it anyway. He'd scooped Earl Bob from winning that ticket. Too bad he couldn't rub his nose in it.

He took the newspaper into the house and dropped it on the kitchen table. Pouring himself a shot of bourbon, he sat down and unrolled the front page. He smiled at the banner photo of Howard holding a giant check. But he gagged on the whiskey when he read the headline.

"Local man wins lotto, donates all to charity."

CHAPTER THREE

The Lazy S cheeseburger and fries tasted marginal, but several locals had recommended the town's original greasy spoon. April took a sip from her glass of lemonade, still a little perturbed by her uninterested audience at story time, and plenty perturbed by how Micah had made fun of the only person who had paid attention to her fairytale. That poor gullible man. Howard seemed like such a gentle soul. Even she wouldn't want to fill his head with wild tales – because he'd believe them. However, she *would* have a few words for Micah the next time he came into the library.

What a bummer. He was the cutest guy she'd met in Silverville, and his awkward personality mirrored her own – except she covered hers with wild tales and theatrics in order to fit in. He didn't even try to get along. He was just weird and shy, even attempting to ignore her, something she really hated. Normally, she'd have made him her summer project. Too bad he ended up being a jerk.

The bell over the diner's door rang, and she glanced up. Looked like she'd get the chance to give him a piece of her mind sooner than expected. She waited until Micah chose the booth in the corner and sat down. She grabbed her lemonade and stomped toward him. Dropping into the bench opposite, she glared.

He looked surprised. "What's your problem?"

"You're the problem, Mr. Micah Ley Lines. That poor Howard Beacon believes all that crap you told him about time travel. I enjoy telling a tale now and then, but not to someone like him."

Micah's eyes grew wide. "He told you?"

"You really are a low-life to lie someone like that. And time-travel, of all things. It isn't even possible. Not unless you're made up of just a few photons, and that experiment was only a fraction of a second." *At least that's what the TV show said last month. Or close enough.* "Scientists would need a generator with more power than any on Earth to build a wormhole big enough to transport people."

She noticed him staring over her shoulder, but she was on a roll. "And besides, even if you could go into the past, physicists say you'd split into a different timeline if you changed anything important, maybe even split into a different universe."

Micah cleared his throat. "Uh, hello, Mr. Price."

April whipped around to see a flabby middle-aged man, his face red and veins popping. He pulled a chair from the nearest table, scooted it up to the booth, and sat down.

"You told her?" he thundered.

April looked from one to the other. "You guys are serious."

Except for a quick glance between them, both men remained silent.

"You really think you can time travel!" April nearly shrieked the words. Other people in the café turned to them at the outburst.

The fat guy slid into the seat beside Micah, leaned forward, and whispered, "I would appreciate you keeping your voice down, young lady." He sat back and looked at Micah. "What does she know?"

"Nothing, I swear!"

April couldn't let it go. The covert glance, the ambiguous behavior – something was going on and she meant to discover it all. She scooted to the edge of her seat and cupped her hands around her mouth. "If you guys don't tell me what you're up to, everyone in the Lazy S is going to hear *my* version of this story in thirty seconds."

At this, the veins in the old guy's forehead extended even further. A tiny glob of sweat at Micah's hairline began to eek its way down his cheek.

"Oh my God, no telling what she'll come up with," Micah groaned.

"Who is this?" the man asked Micah, but his eyes, black and ominous, stayed on April.

If this arrogant ass hoped to intimidate her, he was wrong. She could play that game, too. Her lizard contacts could only help. "April," she answered with an edge of menace. "April Schauers." Then, for extra emphasis, she added, "I can be your best friend or your worst enemy."

From the look of his face, maybe the man was about to laugh; maybe he intended to thump her across the head right there in the café. Whatever he meant to do, he squirmed in his seat and then jumped up with surprising speed, considering his heft.

"C'mon, we're having this conversation at my house. Now. You, too, Miss Schauers."

THIS club was getting too big. Micah fretted over the addition of the obnoxious girl. All he wanted was access to the outhouse, particularly to go back and visit Sarah – regardless of the Puritan customs he had so misunderstood on his last Day Trip.

But Puritan times had another attraction beside Sarah. Despite the humiliation of having her preacher-father stick him in stocks in the middle of the village commons, Micah had to admit

51

he kind of admired some of their rules. They seemed to have a stronger sense of right and wrong than anybody he'd ever been around. Sure was a change from all the do-it-if-it-feels-good routine he got from his mother and her latest loser boyfriend. No, the Puritans weren't like that. They had reasons for doing – and not doing – stuff. And he envied their clear-cut rules. A "strong moral compass," one of the books he'd read on them had called it.

But what hope did he have of getting back for a visit to Puritan times now that more and more people had gotten involved? Buford Price was bad enough, and now it looked like this nosey, pushy girl April wasn't going to go away any time soon.

So here he sat with Mr. Big Shot and Miss Nosey-Pushy around the Price kitchen table.

Unbelievably, Buford must have just noticed April's lizard contacts.

"What's wrong with your eyes, girl?" he asked her.

She bent over the table and popped out the lenses, replacing them with a pair of eight-ball contacts. Micah caught a glimpse of her true eye color. Green, almost turquoise.

"I want to hear about the time travel," she demanded.

A tense, silent moment passed.

"What we say can't leave this room," Buford said.

"I can live with that."

Buford shrugged and nodded to Micah, who told her about his experiences over the past few weeks, how he time-traveled and why he thought the fungus, combined with the ley lines, made it possible.

April sat back, a slight frown on her face, as though she had trouble wrapping her head around the whole notion. At last, she turned to him and said, "My God, you're serious. You weren't messing with Howard's head."

"I'd never do that to Howard."

Her gaze stayed on him and she smiled. "I'm really glad to hear that."

"It's only your consciousness that can travel," Micah continued. "There's no easy explanation for it, but the best I've come up with is the ancient Egyptian belief that what they called the Ka can leave and travel around. Your body stays behind."

"It's not the Ka but the Ba that leaves the body," April corrected. "The Ba is closer to what we call a soul. The Egyptians thought the Ka was the life force but the Ba was more like our personality."

Micah continued to explain, "But the problem is, at least in the outhouse, a person can't seem to control just exactly where the Ba will land, who the receptacle will be. It's like possessing somebody else for a day. You take them over when they're asleep."

Buford snorted. "I sure found that out the hard way."

So had Micah, multiple times. His Day Trips had landed him in lots of awkward situations. But every time he traveled, he learned more. It's why the outhouse had to be saved. He had to make Buford understand. There was no hope now of keeping the experience just for himself with the cat – or the Ba –out of the bag.

The phenomenon had the potential to be world-changing. Maybe it would be possible to stop Hitler from coming into power, or prevent terrorists from crashing planes into the Twin Towers. The capacity to make the world a better place was staggering. But then, April had said changing the past just split events into different timelines. Well, they'd never know if Buford destroyed the outhouse. Would he even get it?

"You know, Mr. Price, you have to keep the outhouse intact."

Buford started to interrupt, but Micah kept talking. "And here's why. The outhouse somehow catches and holds the life force until the Ba comes back. If you plan on time-traveling again, you'll need the outhouse."

"Already decided not to tear it down. Got big plans for my own little time machine."

All the while, April had sat listening. But then she ventured, "Why limit it to *your* little time machine?"

Both men looked at her, waiting for her to continue.

She stood and began to pace around the kitchen. "Think about it. All through the ages people have wanted to time-travel. So turn it commercial."

Micah was horrified, particularly when he looked at Buford and saw the wheels start to turn.

"You mean charge people to use it?" Buford asked.

"Yeah, but you said yourself you both ran into problems. You're going to need a history consultant to prevent those nasty little faux pas in a culture you're not familiar with. I, of course, can help with that. History is what I know."

"Whoa!" Micah spewed. "This is just wrong. Maybe we should be telling scientists – maybe even world leaders – about all this."

Buford slammed his hand on the table. "Don't be a fool. There's money to be made here." He turned to April. "Brilliant. Consider yourself a partner."

"Deal. Maybe I'll try time-traveling, too."

Micah nodded, miserable at the thought of his outhouse becoming a marketable enterprise. "Yeah, anyone who goes into the outhouse can."

AS HE downshifted to help his old pickup make the hill, Grady O'Grady felt the first dangerous rumblings about belt level. The night before, he and Leona had eaten at the Hangar 18 hamburger joint, and now that second order of curly fries didn't sit right.

Making his mood even worse, the elk-scouting trip had been a bust. Just about everywhere he had searched that day, he'd run into picnickers, bicyclers, and four-wheelers. Enough to scare all the wildlife away. Damn, Silverville was getting crowded.

And not with decent people, either.

The crazies started flocking to the area a few years back. They called it a UFO mecca after Howard saw some lights in the woods. Maybe UFOs came to town, maybe not. Either way Grady figured it was a crackpot mecca now.

Seemed like a slur on the valley's proud heritage of mining and ranching – a legacy passed on, in part, by his great-great grandpappy Fergal and his great-great grandma Ada. Unlike the current sheriff, who turned a blind eye to all sorts of foolishness, Grandpappy cleaned up Silverville's 1870s' boomtown days. Now *there* was a man's man, and one who never took any guff from riffraff.

They'd even erected a plaque at the courthouse in honor of the day Sheriff O'Grady gunned down the notorious Black Jack Baker, the town's previous lawman. Folks had said shooting Black Jack was the best thing that ever happened. The way the story passed down, the rough frontier town hired Baker to keep peace after he'd shot and killed three rowdies during a card game. Wasn't long after that the townsfolk realized they had made a mistake but, by then, they couldn't get rid of him. The man bullied and beat up half the population – when he wasn't dunk and whoring. Fergal was the only one brave enough to stand up against him. He killed the son-of-a-bitch in a high-noon Main Street showdown, earning a badge and the town's respect.

About the time Grady reached the old Ketchem place – the one Buford Price had recently bought – he felt the second rumbling from his gut, more explosive than the first. He realized he wasn't going to make it all the way home, and this wasn't something a trip behind sagebrush would take care of.

Then he remembered the outhouse behind the Ketchem's barn. He stomped on the brakes and turned the pickup down the drive.

He skidded to a stop, wrenched the door open, and hightailed past the barn as he tugged his belt buckle loose. Hobbling into the outhouse, he plopped his backside over the hole and sighed with relief.

Good thing Grandpappy didn't eat curly fries the day he killed Baker.

COLD water slapped his face and flew up his nose. Grady coughed and gagged as he felt a rough yank on his hair pulling back his head.

"You got 'til noon to come up with that dollar fifty."

Through slits of swollen eyelids, Grady could just make out a large-headed man with a wide handlebar moustache who barked at him within inches of his face, breath sour and hot.

The man ground Grady's face into the floor plankings. While the son-of-a-bitch unlocked the ankle shackles, Grady looked up to see a pair of expensive boots supporting a stout bull of a fellow wearing a shiny sheriff's star pinned to the lapel of his vest.

He hadn't quite staggered to his feet when he felt a powerful blow on his backside that booted him out the door, past a boardwalk, and face down on a dusty old pile of horse manure. Spurs clanked behind him, and that same powerful voice boomed, "No using whores on credit. 'Specially Ada."

Grady stood and ran his hands over his face. Blood oozed from where he should have found two front teeth.

"I mean it, Gopher. Noon. Or you'll answer to *this*," the voice snarled. The unmistakable cock of a revolver clicked into place.

Then the laughter, from both sides of the street. Strangers, mostly men, stared down at Grady, their shabby clothes covered in grime. Some sported moustaches like the foul-tempered lawman. Others wore full beards that hid their throats.

Directly in front of him on the opposite side of the street stood a newly erected storefront, its board siding green and unpainted. A sign stretched over the door: "Silverville Mercantile – Groceries-Liquor-Cigars."

Grady spun in a circle, taking in the buildings surrounding the street. Didn't look like home to him.

What the hell is going on?

Like the mercantile, the other few structures appeared fairly new. The closest was clearly a blacksmith shop. A man wearing an apron bent over an anvil, hammering at his work. Orange sparks flew with each strike, some hitting the ground littered with shovels, chisels, and partially forged drills. The smithy paused, looked up at Grady, and shook his head.

"No odd jobs for you today, Gopher," he shouted, his attention returning to pound the soft, hot metal.

The cluster of men who had ridiculed Grady seemed to lose interest and sauntered in the direction of the largest building on the street, The Silver Dollar Saloon, according to the sign.

As soon as he read the words, he felt thirsty for a shot of whiskey. The kind of gut-tug hankering that comes about from a lifetime of likker. Grady recognized the signs from his younger years, when he'd come dangerously close to regular AA membership. Funny such a craving could be so strong in a dream. And this *was* a dream. One that felt too goddam real.

He needed to wake up. Walking over to a horse trough beside a hitching post, he dunked his head into the brackish water for a full thirty seconds. He straightened back up and saw the same dingy town.

Sandwiched in between the three or four storefronts were canvas tents set up willy-nilly down the length of the street. Outside one tent, a woman wearing a long skirt squeezed water from a wad of clothes over a tub. When she noticed him staring, she stopped and motioned him over.

Grady stood without moving. Did she mean him?

Impatient, she hollered, "Gopher, get your ass over here, and I'll give you a penny for refilling this wash tub."

He poked his hands into the pockets of his coarse wool pants. Empty. A penny would get him started toward his dollar fifty, and he began to shuffle over.

Wait a minute, what the hell am I doing? Who cared about the dollar fifty? In a few minutes, Leona would wake him up with a breakfast of flapjacks and bacon.

At that moment, rubbery lips nipped at this sleeve. He jumped around to bump into the muzzle and long ears of a haltered mule; a pair of loaded-down panniers balanced on either side of the animal's withers. Just like the six mules strung out behind it. The pack train's muleskinner shoved him to the side.

"Get out of the way, bummer! These mules don't take it kindly when fellers block their way to the assay office."

Grady stepped aside and watched the animals mindlessly trudge toward a small building at the far end of the street.

Yep, they sure as hell smelled like mules. Could you smell mule shit in a dream? Maybe he needed that drink after all.

He crossed the road, stepped up onto the boardwalk, and headed into the saloon. Making his way up to the bar, he ordered a whiskey, but the bartender refused.

"You used up your credit." With that, the barkeep turned away.

Voices from the back invited him to join a game of faro. "Or did you lose all your money last night?" one asked. Laughter rang out around the table, and then the card players also turned their backs.

Grady was about to leave when he heard a female voice above him. He looked up to see a woman with tousled red hair coming down a staircase, struggling to pull up the strap of her petticoat. A little on the plump side but striking.

She hurried down the last few steps and led him to an empty table in the corner. Leaning in close, she whispered, "Fergal, you don't look so good."

"Pardon me, ma'am? I don't rightly know who you are."

She creased her eyebrows and studied his face. "Dang it! Black Jack must have knocked the sense out of you. It's me, Ada."

A greasy looking drunk staggered up to the woman and dropped a silver coin between her breasts. "What'll that buy me upstairs, darlin'?"

She twisted him in the other direction and gave him a push. "Nothing right now, I reckon. Ask one of the other girls." She didn't bother to return the coin; the drunk didn't notice.

Fergal? Ada? He thought for a moment and then slapped his knee and let out a full-bellied guffaw. What a crazy, crazy dream.

"I really need that drink."

"No, what you need is a dollar fifty. By noon."

GRADY dragged his battered body down the street to tell the washer woman he'd be happy to refill her tubs for a penny. As long as he was stuck in this dream, he might as well humor Ada. He shook his head. How he'd gotten the notion his great-great grandma worked as a whore, he'd never know. Dreams sure were funny that way. Or maybe it was the curly fries.

Stepping up on the boardwalk in front of the mercantile, he caught a glimpse of himself in the windowpane. Damn, what an ugly cuss. Hair every which way, black eyes, and a shirt covered with stains and blood – all attached to a short, skinny frame.

In no way did the dream-Fergal and the dream-Ada resemble the people in the one picture he had of his great-great grandparents. That photo showed a dignified couple, clearly pillars of the community.

Overhead, the sun had climbed about halfway toward noon, and he spent the rest of the morning dredging up odd jobs that earned him exactly eleven more cents. Not that he worried much. People didn't get gunned down and die in dreams.

The people and the town turned out pretty much as he expected during Silverville's early days. Folks mostly seemed to work for the major mining operation, The Lucky Star. Women were scarce except for the washer woman and prostitutes. Likely these were tales he'd heard growing up and had just forgotten. What surprised him most in the dream was his keen sense of smell. The street stank of horse shit and the men, including him, smelled like soap hadn't been invented yet.

By the time the shadow disappeared around the horse tank, Ada found him shoveling manure into a wheelbarrow outside the blacksmith shop and livery. This time, she wore more than a petticoat, and rhinestone combs held up her hair. She carried a small basket filled with chicken legs and cornbread.

"Best be eating something, Fergal." She shielded her eyes against the noonday sun. "I hope it won't be your last meal."

Grady pushed the shovel into the wheelbarrow and walked with her to the boardwalk, where they sat down to eat.

"How much so far?" she asked.

He reached into his pocket and pulled out the handful of pennies.

She sighed. "Damn, wish I could help you some, but Black Jack took everything I earned last night." She pulled up the folds of her skirt and tugged loose a small two-shot derringer from a red garter. "I can give you this, though."

"Everything's just plum crazy. I won't be needing no gun."

She placed the tiny firearm in his hands and looked over his shoulder toward the jail house. "Yes, you will."

Grady scooted around to follow her gaze.

BLACK Jack jangled down the street, his spurs leaving a narrow trail in the dirt with each stride. He swore and spat at the onlookers who emerged out of nowhere to watch the showdown as he progressed toward Grady and Ada.

Dropping his chicken leg with one hand and shoving Ada to the side with the other, Grady stood to face him. But he still wasn't worried. Not much, anyway.

The lawman stopped about twenty yards away and cupped his hand over his six-shooter's holster. "Better have that dollar fifty on you, Gopher!"

Grady turned his head toward Ada. "Why do people keep calling me Gopher, anyway?"

She shrugged. "Cuz I reckon all you've ever been good at is goin' and fetchin'."

He started to laugh. He laughed so hard he had to bend over to catch his breath. As he did so, a bullet whizzed past his ear. Damn. Dream or not, that son-of-a-bitch meant to kill him. Instinctively, Grady fell to ground, rolled and aimed his wee palm pistol at the sheriff. He fired.

A small puff of dust materialized ten feet away. For a second, Black Jack looked at the bullet-size crater. Then he roared into action and ran toward Grady, bellowing like a just-branded beefalo.

"Run!" Ada shouted.

Grady couldn't believe his arthritic knees could move so fast. He sprang to his feet and skedaddled toward the livery, his boots drumming the ground as he knocked down the smithy and sent his forge flying. Hot coals rolled across the floor, forcing Grady to hopscotch his way to the back of the building. Clutching a hammer hanging on a nearby wall, he continued to run through an aisle of stalls and out a large sliding door.

Another shot rang out, lodging itself in the boards of a corral fence. Black Jack managed to follow right behind him. Grady dodged to the left at the side of the building and collided with a wooden staircase leading to another level. He looked up. There was no second floor. Another shot careened past his head, and he loped up the steps anyway, two at a time. Sure as hell didn't seem like a dream chase, where running felt like slogging through water.

Once he reached the top, he looked around. Damn if this building didn't even have a roof – only a canvas stretched across the top. He heard Black Jack scuffing up the stairs behind him and decided to take the only course of action available. He jumped onto the canvas.

He had only been on a trampoline one other time in his life. He neither liked it nor ever wanted to try it again. His jumping partner, another tot at his country school, made sure Grady bounced twice as high by jumping and landing just as Grady's feet hit the surface. It even sent him clear over the edge to hit the ground hard.

The recollection gave him an idea.

Black Jack topped the last step, turned, and took aim. Grady began a furious fit of jumping all over the canvas roof.

"Hold still so I can kill ya!" the sheriff demanded. Several times he took a shot but couldn't hit his bouncing quarry.

Grady grinned back, jumping in every direction. As he'd hoped, Black Jack fell for the bait and threw himself onto the canvas. Grady waited until the lawman made his first bounce and soared high, and then Grady managed a mighty spring. Just after Black Jack landed, so did Grady one second later, in turn tossing the bastard six feet into the air. He landed with impressive force, but he didn't fly up and over the roof, as Grady intended. Instead, the sheriff landed hard enough to shove his spurs right into the canvas. He struggled but he was caught fast.

"Goddam you, Gopher!" Black Jack shouted. "Now look what you've . . ."

62

Grady heard a loud ripping sound and Black Jack sank out of sight. He bounced over to the hole and peered down, but before he could get a good look at anything, the canvas split wider, swallowing him and his hammer, too.

He felt a soft bundle under him as he landed, but his head didn't fare as well. As he rolled off the body that broke his fall, his head hit an anvil, nearly knocking him silly. He staggered to his feet and glanced at Black Jack, lying face down. He raised the hammer to strike, but the sheriff was already dead, a hoof file poking through his back.

Behind him, he heard clapping and cheering. Someone called out, "By God, Gopher, you got rid of that bastard!"

Ada threw herself at him, wrapping her arms around his chest. "You're the town hero, Fergal."

He leaned over and clutched her shoulders for support, but his knees collapsed as he passed out.

"WHAT the hell are you doing?" Buford barked. He peeled Grady's hands off his shoulders and shook the old rancher out of his groggy state.

Grady blinked several times and stared at Buford like he didn't even recognize him. "Seemed so real. Crazy dream."

But Buford knew exactly what had happened. He pulled Grady off the one-seater and tugged him outside to lean against the wall. "Must have hit your head. Why were you in my outhouse?"

"Why the hell do you think I was in there?" Grady hitched up his belt. "Too many curly fries."

Kicking the outhouse door shut, Buford led him toward the pickup, opened the door, and shoved Grady inside. He wanted to make sure the rancher left before he had a chance to start asking questions. Better Grady drove off thinking he'd had some sort of nightmare.

"Not sure I can drive yet." Grady rubbed his forehead.

Buford leaned over him and turned the key in the ignition. "Sure you can."

He stood back and watched the pickup truck weave down the driveway and turn toward Silverville.

This is bad, real bad. He couldn't have folks wandering in off the road and using the outhouse – not for free.

First thing that morning, he'd call Bob to delay bulldozing the shack. And he'd explore other options for changing the property into a commercial time-travel venture rather than a shooting range. April had been right. The outhouse held bigger potential than his own personal use. Why, he could manipulate events in the past to make money. What he hadn't thought about, until he found Grady, was how to protect his investment. Maybe before he did anything else, he'd have a perimeter fence built around the whole place. Add some guard dogs.

He'd need to make an appointment with a lawyer to talk about drafting liability release forms for clients taking Day Trips. The sign would have to change from "Price's Shooting Paradise" to "Price's Day Trip Paradise." No, something snappier, with alliteration. What was it Micah had called the soul, the Ba? Maybe "Buford's Ba Trips." The boy had said the bodies of people in the past actually caught the Ba of the Day Tripper. So maybe "Ba Catchers" would be better. Or even "Ka Catchers." Those kids had mentioned that word as well. He couldn't remember exactly what it meant, but the name "Ka Catchers" had a nicer ring. He'd call the sign company right away.

For the time being, he needed to keep Micah and April involved, Micah to prevent him from blabbering about the outhouse to scientists and world leaders. Besides, the kid had a handle on how this thing worked and could maybe refine the process to give it more control. April was a different story – she was sharp, ambitious, a lot like himself. And she knew about history, which could be useful guiding clientele to safe places that would minimize the operation's liability.

Even more important, they were kids and would probably work for minimum wage.

Buford was going to make a bundle.

CHAPTER FOUR

April rested her chin on her hand and stared at Buford, who sat across the table beside Micah. With her other hand, she swiped at sawdust floating in the air from the construction work at the old ranch house where they huddled. Finally she spoke. "But it's the Ba, not the Ka that leaves the body."

"Ka, Ba, Schma." Buford waved a hand through the air. "Who cares? Who around here is ever gonna know the difference?"

"Who around here?" April asked. "Maybe not too many, but we're planning on national attention. You'll sound like an idiot." She shot a quick wink at Micah, but he didn't, or wouldn't, respond.

"It's Ka Catchers. I'm the CEO of this little operation and that's what I decided. End of discussion."

April sighed and moved her eyes down the page of meeting notes. Maybe Buford wasn't entirely an idiot – he did, after all, recognize her talents and agree to bring her aboard, and he had been the one to initiate Alien Landing theme park, one of the biggest moneymakers in town. But not all of his ideas had turned green. Price's Ski Paradise turned into a bust after the first year.

Since accepting his junior partner offer a week ago, she'd spent some time digging into his past, finding bits of information in public records and newspaper articles. She also managed to drop his name on people who came into the library. April had pieced together a mixed picture of part genius and part fool (depending on who you asked), a sometimes-successful businessman, and a mildly miserable divorcee whose ex-wife looked ill whenever his name popped up. Most agreed he bragged too much and often skirted the truth. April could live with that, as long as he didn't recognize that same fluke in her.

"Okay, we're down to the part that lists job descriptions." Buford's obnoxious voice brought her back to the agenda.

She scanned hers first. "Counselor? I'm a Day Trip counselor?"

"Of course," Buford answered. "You're the one who knows all about history. I'm thinking you could pick out maybe six or so safe time periods for people to visit. You know, cut back on any chance of liability."

She mentally considered the possibilities. There weren't many, certainly not six. Offhand she could think of a few – Rome in the first couple centuries A.D., the Mongol Empire under Ghengis Khan, and Japan before they let in Europeans. Not much else she could remember from her history books. But those were still dangerous times by modern standards. No vaccines, inadequate food supplies, poor hygiene. And safe only because punishment was harsh. Fear kept people in line. The only other time she could think of was post-World War Two America, but how could she talk everyone into going there?

"What if they have someplace else in mind?" April asked.

"What?" Buford cupped an ear to lessen the whine from the drill in the next room.

She leaned across the table and shouted, "They might want to go someplace else."

The drilling stopped.

"That's what this release form is for." Buford held up a document full of legal jargon and blank lines for signatures. "Can't be too careful."

Her job description seemed a lot denser than Micah's or Howard's. Looks like she might have to drop her library internship that summer if she wanted to be part of this venture. Maybe change her major to travel and recreation management when she returned to school in the fall. She read over the specifics of her duties for Ka Catchers. *Oversee travelogue presentations, help set up TV commercials, offer client briefings before and after each day trip, keep wardrobe facility equipped. . .* the list covered half a page.

"Wait a second," she said. "What's with the wardrobe facility? You're not planning on costuming clients, are you? It's not like they can travel in period attire."

"Hey, if looking the part helps sell, why not?"

Finally Micah cleared his throat and spoke. "So my job involves taking people to the outhouse and staying there until they come back?"

"It makes sense, boy. You know better than anyone how this thing works."

Micah's eyes scanned the notes, and he began shaking his head. "What the hell? No, I won't paint the outhouse or install air fresheners."

"Folks will be paying good money, LOTS of money to use that outhouse. We don't want them gagging when they – "

"That could change the whole dynamics. Without – "

"Dammit Micah! Who's the CEO here?"

April watched the argument persist for five minutes. Yes, Buford certainly was part fool. Paint could very well kill the fungus which, in turn, could kill the business. She stood and interrupted them.

"I'll prepare clients for the smell during the Day Trip briefings. And maybe we could plant flowers along the outhouse perimeter to distract from its, ah, appearance."

Both men seemed satisfied with her idea.

Micah cleared his throat. "How will Ho –" he broke into a coughing fit, raising his hand so they'd wait until he finished.

Buford peered closely at him. "My God, boy, what's wrong with you? You look pale as my lily white ass."

April looked at Micah, too. He didn't look healthy. Too much time in front of a computer screen?

"Sorry, let's try that again," Micah wheezed. "How will Howard like his job titles?"

Buford paused, maybe to see if Micah was through coughing. He picked something green out of his teeth, examined it, and popped the morsel back in his mouth, swallowing. "You mean coffee executive and chief custodian? I've already told him. He's delighted."

A workman approached the table and said, "You guys need to move. We're about to pull down this ceiling."

The Ka Catcher team gathered their materials and retreated outside.

April asked Buford, "I assume you have new plans for the old ranch house now that you've bagged the shooting range?"

He jerked a thumb over his shoulder at the building. "We'll use the living room space as an entry with posters, displays, and such to hype the Day Trips. It'll be the travelogue presentation room for slide shows, too."

They walked to Buford's car, where he opened the trunk and handed out three folding chairs he'd "borrowed" from Fine Funeral Home as temporary furniture. They arranged them in the driveway.

Buford turned to April. "I'm thinking the two biggest upstairs bedrooms will be offices for me and you. Micah and Howard won't need 'em. And the little bedroom for wardrobe and dressing area."

"I want the biggest one," she asserted.

Buford frowned. "I'm the CEO and I should get –"

"You don't want to look like a cheapskate, cramming the travelers and their families into a cramped room while I prep them."

"But I –"

"Besides, that bedroom has the west-facing window for clients to look out at the outhouse."

All three turned to stare at the ramshackle privy.

Buford sighed. "Mmm, I don't think a few flower pots are gonna cut it." He puckered his lips for a moment. "What we need is a more inviting façade. You know, one that looks like it came out of a Flash Gordon movie." He turned to Micah. "You're into computers. Search sites online and come up with some ideas."

"Think of the name, Buford," April broke in. "It's Ka Catchers; it better have an Egyptian theme."

"Okay, *you* design it. Maybe leave room for a few seasonal touches. Holiday trips during Thanksgiving and Christmas."

"Whoa!" Micah raised his palms to stop Buford's train of thought. "We can't run this in the winter time."

"Why not?"

"The fungus could become dormant in cold weather. We don't know if it will even work then. And people's bodies would freeze while they're waiting for their Ba to come back."

Buford's mouth fell open in horror. "My God, boy. Why didn't you mention this before? You mean I'm sinking all this money into the operation, and I can only run it five months out of the year?"

Christ on a corndog, Buford. How far into the future do you think, anyway? April to the rescue again. It was already becoming a pattern. She lowered her head and scratched a couple of quick

70

calculations on paper. Between now, the middle of June, to the end of September, they might still show a profit by the close of the season. Assuming they jumped right on the advertising, they might start accepting clients as early as mid-July. She pulled out her cell and tapped a few numbers on the calculator app.

"Okay, by the time we get going, we'll have roughly seventy days before we close shop for the winter." She talked as she tapped. "At one client per day, that's seventy travelers. If we charge ten-thousand a crack, we'd gross seven-hundred grand."

Buford whistled in appreciation of the numbers, then stopped. "Ten grand? Sounds kinda pricey. Only rich folks could afford that."

April set down the phone and nodded. "Exactly, rich folks. How else can we ensure people won't go to the past seeking their fortune and changing the future? That would really be an asshole thing to do."

She ignored the odd look on Buford's face, hoping he got her point.

Micah added, "That brings up a whole new can of worms. We'll have to warn people not to do that. Maybe have them sign an affidavit that they won't try to change anything. 'Course, how will we know they'll honor it?"

"I've already thought of that," April said. "In the briefing, I'll warn them about the pitfalls. Like maybe they'll prevent themselves from getting back to the outhouse, or maybe from being born in the first place. That should scare 'em."

"What if they want to go into the future?" Micah asked.

"Already thought of that, too. We'll discourage it. We tell them we can assure their safety in the past because we already know what happened. Can't do that for the future."

She waited for Buford's input, but he looked as though he was lost in his own mental calculations.

"Buford, anything to add to this?"

"Seven-hundred grand, minus three percent for each of you, and a one-and-a-half percent for Howard... that's six-hundred and fifty grand for the first season."

"No," April replied.

"No?"

"Fifteen percent for me, ten for Micah, five for Howard. And we get health benefits and base pay."

"Wait a minute!" Buford blustered.

"You have almost no overhead except for the initial expense of putting the operation together. And you'll recoup that investment during this first season, plus you'll come out with at least twenty-five percent. And next year" – she grabbed the phone calculator again – "you'll have four-and-a-half months. Enough time for 135 travelers. You'll be a millionaire."

Buford's eyes glazed over, but he snapped back in seconds. "Your pay scales are still too high."

"You're lucky that's all it is. You can't run this business by yourself, and Micah and I will be doing most of the work. If you don't like it, bring in someone else. But every day lost is ten-thousand dollars to you."

He scowled and grumbled, his complaints sputtering out.

April continued, "There are other reasons I need that money. Twice a year I have to fly to Switzerland for my shots. And they're eight grand a pop."

"Huh?"

"For the Uruguayan Flying Worm Syndrome. When I was a little girl, my parents..."

MICAH had almost called in sick that morning. He couldn't seem to shake the summer flu.

A little wobbly, he squatted and plucked a blade of grass to chew. By now, he could recite Buford's lines by heart. Thankfully, the film production company in charge of the commercial decided to change the intro scene where Buford was supposed to hold a horse.

Creative Solutions had filmed for four days, and it didn't look like the thirty-second spot had moved any closer to completion. Buford had hired the same folks who'd shot the movie *Silverville vs. the Flying Saucers* a couple summers ago. For the Ka Catchers' project, they arrived with a full assortment of props and costumes tailored to the three Day Trips Buford wanted to feature.

But they didn't bring a horse. That prop came from a local who got wind of the film crew in town and showed up to be an extra. But all they wanted was her horse. Unfortunately, she'd never trained it to work in front of cameras.

After a dozen unsuccessful takes of the intro, the owner led the big black and white pinto troublemaker temporarily off the set while Buford gave his on-camera spiel about Ka Catchers. Now a crew member stood off camera on a stool dropping reins down into Buford's hand, so it looked like he held the horse.

Yesterday's shooting went pretty well. In the morning, Micah, April, and Buford – the "talent" – had dressed as Pilgrims and Howard as a Wampanoag chief for a short vignette about the first Thanksgiving. Candace B. Good, the director, would add voice-over during post-production editing. Micah recited the only line, "My Ka Catcher is a Pilgrim," while everyone pretended to eat fake food.

In the afternoon they shot a scene of April as a slinky Egyptian princess eating grapes dropped into her mouth by Mark Antony, played by Micah. She sure got pissed off when she'd seen the skimpy outfit Buford had picked out. It may not have been authentic, as April complained, but Micah thought she looked really hot in the costume. He wasn't *that* sick. What would a girl like that do if a guy like him asked her out? Laugh. The idea turned his stomach into knots. Then again, maybe…

73

Howard walked over and dropped down on the grass beside Micah to watch Buford's close-up for the current scene.

Clutching dangling reins in one hand and a ten-foot jousting lance in the other, Buford began to speak. "Come on down for the best deal on time travel. It's the *only* deal on time trav –"

The visor on his helmet clapped shut and the director shouted, "Cut! Buford, you've got to hold still while you talk."

Buford raised his gauntleted hand to lift the visor. "Well, that's pretty damn hard in this itchy armor." He struggled to reach his armpit and tried to scratch.

"If we hadn't had to add those burlap extensions on the side for your, uh, girth, your outfit wouldn't *be* so itchy," the director replied.

Howard leaned over to Micah and whispered, "Is Mr. Price going to get on the horse pretty soon?"

Micah glanced over at the fidgeting steed dancing circles around its owner. Good question. With any luck, Buford would get bucked off, conk his head, and wouldn't remember anything about the outhouse. So far, no one took Buford's latest scheme seriously anyway. Except April. He still couldn't get the vision of her in the Egyptian costume out of his head.

He didn't understand why she was involved in all this, why she didn't see the bigger picture, the scientific value of the outhouse. Now look where it was all going. He regretted telling Buford in the first place, but he'd had to.

Buford managed to get through the next take without any wardrobe malfunctions. The director scribbled notes on her tablet and called out. "Time to mount up."

Even with the helmet half obscuring Buford's face, Micah could see sweat pouring down the knight's cheeks. Or maybe they were tears.

"Can't we use a stunt double for this?" Buford asked.

Candace prodded him along. "Not on the budget you gave us." She shouted over her shoulder, "Bring the horse."

The owner dodged dancing hooves as the animal dragged her in reluctant zigzags toward the cameras. "Her name is Annalee."

"Whatever."

Annalee's owner gave her horse to the handlers and stepped to the side, next to Micah.

"What's with all the old costumes?" she asked.

"Filming shots for Ka Catchers. We're going to give people a chance to go into the past."

"You mean like some sort of virtual reality theme park?"

"Not exactly," Micah hedged. Buford didn't want them talking about the operation to the public until they had the publicity campaign ready. "Excuse me."

He walked over to get a closer view of the film crew's preparations.

Once the horse, held fast by its bridle, stood before the camera, the crew placed a mounting block below the saddle and guided Buford into position. He used his toe to nudge aside the blanket hiding the western gear underneath and pushed his boot into the stirrup. With a mighty grunt, he started to heave himself up. At that moment, Annalee swung to the side, pitching Buford forward to tumble onto the ground in a metal heap.

The director shouted, "Get more help over here!"

Two men raised Buford to his feet and led him back to the mounting block. The owner occupied Annalee with horse cookies while Micah and two others shouldered the steed back to her mark.

"Hold her there," Candace ordered, "and keep that camera angle tight."

Crew members held the horse in place while Buford made it into the saddle.

After four seconds of footage showing the knight's successful mounting, the director stopped filming and waited for the next shot. She walked over to Buford and said, "Now before you gallop away, remember to say, "My Ka Catcher is King Arthur.""

She motioned everyone to back away and gave the order to release the horse. But for once, Annalee stood quietly, savoring the last remnants of her cookies.

"Somebody slap that horse!" Candace commanded.

Micah approached, but instead of smacking the hindquarters, he pulled a pencil from his pocket and jabbed her in the rump. Like the knight's charger she was meant to portray, Annalee reared and bolted forward. Buford's screams echoed off the hills as he and his mount disappeared down the road.

The boom-mic operator lowered his rig. "He never said –"

Candace waved her hand. "Oh hell, I'm not shooting this again. We'll dub it in."

BUFORD tugged down his Roman tunic and straightened the wreath on his head. He grimaced at his bare, plump legs exposed beneath his garment like the drumsticks of an undercooked turkey. The guests for Ka Catchers' open house would arrive soon. He made one last sweep around the remodeled facility to make sure everything was in order. Caterers arranged trays of fruit and hors d'oeuvres and filled the coffee urns at either ends of the long tables. Helium-filled balloons on long red and blue ribbons bobbed about the room.

He studied his watch and turned to the stairs. Where were those guys? Probably still fussing with their costumes. Buford and Micah had teased April when they'd all gathered that morning to look through the wardrobe, telling her she should wear the Cleo outfit again, but Creative Solutions had taken that back to Hollywood after the shoot a couple weeks earlier. She'd ignored them and opted for a more conservative Queen Elizabeth look, complete with high ruffled collar. Micah had chosen a Pilgrim costume – not as good as the one from the film company, but Buford figured no one would know the difference.

He barked orders to the caterers and kicked a stray strawberry under the cloth covering one table. A ruckus from the top of the staircase caught his attention, and he looked in time to see Howard rolling down the steps, arms flailing, Persian kaftan billowing. Good thing he wore a turban to absorb the shock when his head slammed against the hardwood floor at the bottom.

Waiters at that moment entering with an ice sculpture almost dropped their masterpiece and rushed to Howard.

"He's all right!' Buford boomed. "Get that sculpture to the center of the room."

April skipped down the stairs, Micah dragging behind her, concern on both their faces when they saw Howard propped against the wall trying to rewrap his turban.

"What happened?" April asked.

"Nothing. Okay, last briefing before the guests arrive." Buford motioned his team to huddle around him. "April, you sit at the desk in the corner, taking trip reservations. We're gonna have loads, so make sure you have several pens. Micah, you mix and mingle with me."

Buford examined the strip of wrapping that dangled from Howard's turban. "You're in charge of picking up empty plates and dumping them in the trashcan."

Out the window, Buford saw the first cars arrive. "Number one priority: Make sure no one gets past that courtyard gate."

One of the first things Buford had construction crews build was a tall wooden perimeter fence around the outhouse. The setup involved a wrought-iron gate allowing people to peer into a courtyard twenty feet deep and see the façade hiding the outhouse. He didn't want to take any chances. Locks protected the wrought-iron gate, the door on the façade, and the outhouse door itself.

The façade, which he insisted they call The Time Portal, had turned out better than he expected. With April's historical expertise and Micah's artistic talent, the project captured the mystique of time travel while keeping the Egyptian theme of Ka Catchers. The apex of the portal depicted a big pyramid, framing a head-on shot of the Sphinx beneath. Paintings of two Egyptian guys wearing little skirts stood on either side of the entrance, each holding up glowing globes. To him they looked like crystal balls, but April explained they represented symbols of time travel. Worked for him, so long as it impressed clients. On either side of The Time Portal stood additional tall wooden walls stretching to the sides of the perimeter fence.

Buford took one last look at his team and signaled Micah to follow him out the door to meet guests. April took her station at the reservation desk. Howard wrestled with opening a large, flat plastic trash bag.

The ranch house front door opened and the first guests filed in.

Buford rushed to the entrance and spread his arms wide. "Welcome to Ka Catchers."

THE FOOD disappeared fast – no thanks to all the freeloading locals, who never stopped at April's reservation desk. That worthless dogcatcher-turned-deputy-sheriff Arno Aasfresser stationed himself next to the hors d-oeuvres table, and he ate the whole plate of stuffed mushrooms before any other guests had a chance to try them. In fact, most of the town trailer trash showed up, people who could never afford a Day Trip.

More promising was the arrival of Chantale Getty-Schwartz with her crackpot albino Indian friend, Hans High Horse. Those two were loaded. She'd come to town not long after Howard's UFO sighting and bought property next to Grady – to the old rancher's chagrin. As usual, she wore ostrich boots, a stretch sequined bodysuit, and an orange boa draped over a cleavage that reached to her rhinestone western belt buckle. He made a mental note to talk to her before she and Hans got away.

Denton and Felicia Fine made an appearance, proprietors of the local funeral home and longtime friends. They weren't potential clients either, but Buford appreciated the show of moral support.

Denton walked over and shook his hand. It had been two years since the undertaker's hip surgery, and he no longer limped at all.

"Congratulations on the new enterprise, Buford." He lowered his voice. "But I've gotta warn you. Not everyone goes along with making Silverville a time-travel portal."

The town always had naysayers, people who had no vision for the potential Buford saw for their community. If it hadn't been for him, Alien Landing Theme Park would still be a pipe dream, and no movie would have featured their fair city as the destination for an interstellar experience. "Screw 'em. We're talking about the wave of the future – and the past."

"Really works, huh?"

"Indeed it does, my friend. Been on a trip myself." Buford crammed a canapé in his mouth. "Better start saving up for yours. Well, gotta mix and mingle."

Buford sauntered over to the window to see Micah standing by a small cluster of people next to the wrought-iron entrance into The Time Portal's courtyard. Someone pointed inside and Micah nodded vigorously. No doubt explaining the wonders that awaited anyone who could cough up ten thousand dollars.

Still looking out the panes, Buford saw a dark stretch limousine with blackened windows pull into the parking lot. That was more like it. The commercials must be attracting the kind of clientele he'd hoped for. The driver emerged from the vehicle and opened the rear passenger door.

"I just signed up for one of those Day Trips!" Chantale moved in front of him, blocking the window. "I'm going when I get back from my shopping trip to Harrod's this September."

Buford had no chance to respond. Her albino companion, who claimed he was the last member from the lost tribe of Juanabee Indians, said to Chantale, "At last, you'll be able to take your place among the ancient court of the Egyptian royalty."

Chantale clasped her hands together. "I can be Nefritis!" she drawled in a thick Texas twang.

"Nefertiti," Hans corrected.

"Going to Egypt, huh?" Buford asked, beaming at the prosperous start of his venture.

The entryway door opened and in stepped an entourage of three strangers in expensive suits. Two of them looked like bodybuilders, and they flanked a smaller man with a dark complexion. Buford hurried to them and offered his most inviting smile – the one that said, *I'm happy you and your pocketbook are here*. He didn't make it within six feet of the short guy before one of the goons shoved him aside and threatened him with a glare.

Buford retreated, his smile withering.

The smaller man placed a hand lightly on his companion's chest. "It's all right, Bentu." His eyes fell on Buford. "My bodyguards are unfamiliar with American customs."

Intimidated by the man's presence and exotic accent, Buford stepped back against the wall, unable to remember his rehearsed sales pitch. Finally, he squeaked, "You feel free to look around." He gestured to the posters on the walls depicting various famous moments in history. "If you have any questions, talk to me or that girl at the reservation desk."

He pointed at April, who was talking to Perry Pantiwycke, one of the few other prospects in town who could well afford their services.

Things were looking up.

Until he saw Perry's wife, Lela. He hated her, and he was pretty sure the feeling was mutual. During the years she'd served as the city's mayor, that woman had consistently opposed every creative idea he'd ever brought to the table. Not only that, every time he opened his mouth at city council meetings she'd tell him to shut up and sit down. The old bat had a lot of nerve. Everyone else in the community recognized him as a valued mover and shaker. Well, almost everyone.

Perry leaned over April's table and took a pen from her hand to sign on the dotted line. As he scribbled, Lela tossed her hands in the air and stomped away, panning the crowd. When she spotted Buford, her eyes narrowed and she marched in his direction.

Buford turned back to the mysterious limousine's new arrivals, pretending he hadn't seen her. But they'd wandered away. He plowed into the crowd, her scolding voice growing louder as she approached.

"Buford Price, you stop right there!"

He ducked his head and felt his cheeks flush as he sensed her standing right behind him. How did she always manage to make him feel like a third-grader ordered to stand in the corner?

Her hand grasped his arm and pulled him around to face her. "What kind of crazy stunt have you cooked up now?"

"This isn't a stunt. It's a legitimate opera –"

"Snake oil! That's all this is, and now you've talked my husband into your scam. Everyone knows you can't time-travel."

He took a deep breath to respond, but she wouldn't give him the chance.

"You've dreamed up some sort of virtual reality scheme, and now you're trying to pass it off as real." Her finger jabbed into his chest. "You should be ashamed of yourself!"

"But this *is* real," he whined.

"Shut up! I don't want to hear your bull. Get out of my sight." Lela stormed back to April's table, probably to talk Perry out of buying a Day Trip.

Buford realized several nearby people must have heard the whole exchange. He mustered the energy to laugh. He hoped he didn't look as shaken as he felt. Shrugging, he said, "Skeptics. What can you do?"

The day progressed with few other disasters, apart from the melting ice sculpture that caused Howard to slip and dump a bowl of punch over a child's head. Buford glad-handed the wealthy and shunned most of the locals. From time to time, he glanced toward April, who sat idle most of the day. And he never had the opportunity to speak to the mysterious guest flanked by bodyguards, who'd left not long after arriving.

By four o'clock in the afternoon, Buford escorted the last attendee out the door. He found a chair and plopped down, his arches throbbing from the Roman sandals he'd worn all day. That tunic had become annoying, too. Every time he'd taken a step, the fabric had ridden up his thighs, forcing him to pull it down every time he took more than a few steps.

Both Micah and Howard collapsed in nearby chairs.

"Where's April?" Buford asked.

Micah jabbed a finger at the ceiling. "Gone upstairs to change."

Buford stretched over to grab the last remaining bacon-wrapped shrimp. He almost had it to his mouth when he noticed a bite taken out. Probably that damn Aasfresser.

April soon returned in jeans and sweatshirt. She carried the reservation book.

"How'd we do?" Buford tossed the shrimp back at the plate.

She handed him the book. Only three names – Chantale Getty-Schwartz, Perry Pantiwycke, and Mr. Smith.

Buford pointed to the third name. "Who's this?"

"That guy with the goons."

Buford felt relieved he hadn't had to jump the Bentu hurdle to make the sale after all. "But who was he?"

"Do we really care?" She waved a check at Buford stamped with the Republic of Yadim.

"When is he coming?"

"In four days. He seemed to be in a hurry. Buford, it's hard for me to sell these trips without going on one myself."

He raised a dismissive hand. "You're too busy right now. But soon."

He hardly noticed the quick glance April and Micah exchanged.

CHAPTER FIVE

Two days before Ka Catchers officially opened for business, Buford flew to Denver to pick up a limo he'd leased for his latest scheme to gouge the clientele – ghost tours.

Micah thought April had come up with a pretty good idea to occupy Day Trippers' families while they waited around for the adventure to end. At first, she'd contacted Mrs. Watson, the Alien Landing museum curator, to get background on local ghost lore. The septuagenarian warmed to the idea and wanted to give the tours herself. But five minutes of talking with her had convinced April the woman would numb her audience with the monotone voice and mechanical gestures.

"We gotta think of somebody else to guide these tours," April had reported. "Hey, how 'bout Perry Pantiwycke? He's high-energy and likable – if he'd take the job."

Buford grumbled there were already enough people on the payroll. "Besides, I don't want Perry's pushy wife hanging around here. She'd find a way to barge in and take things over. One of you should do it."

Micah and April protested at the same time.

"No way!" Micah said. "I can't leave the outhouse while someone's in there. And April can't work day and night."

"Then how about How – "

April put a hand over her boss's mouth and picked up the phone with the other.

While she dialed Perry's number, Buford hissed, "Not on the payroll. Offer him a discount on his Day Trip, but a not very big one. And his wife can't come with him."

The last thing Micah heard before she hung up was, "Yes, Buford said a complimentary trip."

Good thing she'd kept her hand over Buford's mouth.

And a good thing Buford didn't know their plans while he was in Denver for the next twenty-four hours. Originally, Micah had planned to slip away to Puritan New England to look for Sarah, but April wanted to use this opportunity for herself. Micah couldn't argue with the logic.

"Come on, Micah. This'll be the only time I can sneak away for a Day Trip. And I really need the street smarts to do my job. If I'm going to counsel –"

Micah interrupted her. "I get it. I've listened to you preach at Buford for days. I get it, April."

Now with Buford out of the way, Micah and she sat in the Welcome Center while he tried to walk her through the procedure.

She nodded impatiently. "I know all that. It's my job to tell our clients this stuff."

"Oh, right." He felt a twinge of anxiety. April was cocky. And no way to guess what stories she might tell during her Day Trip – or the consequences. "You're not going to scare people with the Uruguayan Flying Worm, are you?" He wouldn't let her answer. "Promise me you'll be just an observer."

She winked. "No, I've got better stories for this trip."

"Where are you going, anyway?"

"Some place off the beaten track. I'm not one to follow the herd."

At that moment, the door opened.

"GOOD morning, Miss Schauers," the stranger said as he walked into Ka Catchers' Welcome Center. He pulled off a wide-billed baseball cap and oversized pair of sunglasses, giving April a slight bow and nodding to Micah.

Only then did April recognize the man. "Mr. Smith, you're two days too early." She looked past him and saw through the window a small red Honda Civic, not the chauffeured black limo he'd first arrived in during the open house.

Their first client had arrived alone, without his burly goons and without his expensive Armani suit. He looked more casual in khakis and a pullover sweater. "I was wondering if perhaps we could move my appointment to today. Unavoidable affairs of state have made two days from now impossible."

This request threw an unexpected kink in April's plans. She glanced at Micah, who shrugged, barely disguising what passed for a grimace.

Buford would be furious if they turned Mr. Smith away. It wasn't as though they weren't ready to offer their first commercial Day Trip. She guessed she could postpone her own time travel to the next day. She turned to Micah. "What time did Buford say he was getting back tomorrow?"

"Sometime in the morning."

Crap. Tomorrow wouldn't work either. She really did believe Buford would allow her to take a Day Trip, but when? The business was starting to pick up. Several people had called to ask about time travel, and she was pretty sure she'd talked a couple of them into making reservations for the coming week. Plus she had presentations at travel shows scheduled in a half dozen cities over the next month – not to mention all the other promotional schemes

Buford seemed to make up on the fly. It looked like she'd lost her best window of opportunity today. Unless...

"Mr. Smith, I'm sure this won't be a problem, but could you excuse us for a moment?" She pulled out a chair and invited him to have a seat.

April motioned for Micah to follow her into an adjoining room. Once inside, she pushed the door nearly shut and ushered Micah to the far wall. "What do you think would happen if two people Day-Tripped at the same time?"

He stared at her for a moment, scratching at the hair behind his ear. "I – I don't know. We've never tried it."

"Not *exactly* at the same time. What if Smith goes first and I go right after him? Can you handle two people in the outhouse?"

Micah shook his head. "This is a bad idea. Smith's Ba could come back to your body, or yours to his."

"I don't think so. Remember, the Egyptians mummified their bodies to help the Ba recognize the right one. It knows where to go. King Tut was buried with two infants, so the priests must have figured that wouldn't be a problem."

"How do we know if those Ba's ever hooked up with the right people?" Micah groaned. "April, *please* don't ask me to do this."

She shushed him. "We don't want Smith to hear us."

Micah started to pace and shake his head.

"Hear me out," she continued. "Regardless of who comes back first, your main responsibility is to the client. If I show up, just usher me out the door and stay with Smith. If he comes back first, don't worry about me. I have a better idea of what to expect, and I won't be as disoriented since I practically live here anyway. This will work. What could go wrong? "

She didn't wait for Micah to argue. She walked across the room and opened the door wide, a smile pasted on her lips. "Okay, Mr. Smith, let's get down to business."

She picked up the clipboard from her reservation desk and sat across from him. She skimmed over the script Buford had insisted she recite to every traveler before entering The Time Portal. To her, the disclosure read like the Miranda rights. *You have the right to travel wherever you wish, so long as that destination complies with Ka Catchers' recommended list of times and places. You have the right to ... etc., etc. ... You do* not *have the right to seek litigation against Ka Catchers in the unlikely event of misadventure.* ..blah, blah, blah.

She passed him the clipboard. "Just sign at the bottom."

He took the form and read over the contents, pen in hand. Following each disclaimer, he paused and looked up. "How can you prevent me from traveling outside the recommended list?"

"You're very astute, Mr. Smith. We recommend certain places for your safety only." She noticed the five-hundred dollar haircut, the Rolex on his wrist, the diamond-studded rings on three fingers. And his mention of *affairs of state.* Combined with the goons and limo from a few days before, she wondered what it all added up to. What did this guy have up his sleeve? She leaned across the desk and pointed to clause No. 7 – the one intended to scare the hell out of anyone contemplating something stupid.

She read aloud, "Any attempt at changing the future might result in the failure of returning to the present, possibly initiating a chain of events that prevents your birth."

He laughed softly. "Relax, I'm not 'contemplating' anything except an uncomplicated escape from the daily stress of official duties." He signed the form and passed it to her.

"Okay, what did you have in mind?"

"Is it really necessary to divulge that information?" He leaned back and steepled his hands.

She found his nonchalance almost unnerving. He seemed neither excited nor anxious – as though his normal life were accustomed to extraordinary events.

"Yes, I'm afraid it is." She was back on script. "Your chosen destination determines the nature of our counseling session. For instance, can you speak the language? Do you know the customs?"

"Ah, I understand. But where I'm going, there's no need to know the language or the customs. Let me explain. My ancestors of long ago were simple peasants. The most significant responsibility in their daily lives was finding the best grazing hills for their goats. My forefathers roamed with their herds through what is now southern Turkey, only speaking to others during clan gatherings."

Nice story, but where did he want to go?

He took a deep breath. "My wish is to recapture such simplicity – if only for a day."

"Okay. Got it." She started to jot notes. *Southern Turkey, goat herder.* "What year did you say that was?"

"Twelve-thousand years ago."

She looked up, unable to keep her mouth closed. "You can trace your lineage back that far?"

"In my family, yes."

She finished her notes, tore it from the clipboard. "Micah! Mr. Smith is ready to go to the outhouse – I mean, The Time Portal."

BUFORD stared out the airplane window as the craft skimmed over metropolitan developments dotting Denver's outskirts. The pre-landing seatbelt signs lit up the console overhead, and the flight attendant made a last sweep through the cabin with a trash bag for empty cups.

Tomorrow morning, he'd drive back to Silverville in a shiny, new limo. It would be another week before the sign folks could add the permanent Ka Catchers logo to the side of the vehicle, but he'd have Micah or April tape something under the windows until then. Hopefully they'd followed his orders to dress Howard in period clothes and parade him around town. April, he could count on. She showed character, the kind he himself possessed. She was bright, ambitious and inventive. Micah, not so much.

Not that the boy wasn't a great asset to the business. He just didn't have a lot of enthusiasm, and his nay-saying had begun to get under Buford's skin. *We should study the outhouse longer before opening it commercially. We need to share this with scientists. Too dangerous to try group Day Trips.* Yadda, yadda. What an old lady. If there was one thing Buford recognized, it was a good business idea.

Too bad everyone in town didn't see it that way. The Silverville County Commissioners had earlier that week summoned him to a meeting to ask about the legitimacy of Ka Catchers. A lot of community folks attended, and a good many didn't seem too keen on the idea.

"Don't we already have enough weirdoes coming here?" one had asked.

"How do we even know it really works?" another complained.

Buford had calmly explained how the appearance of paying Day Trippers would benefit the town. At ten thousand a crack, they had to be wealthy to begin with and would likely distribute their dollars to restaurants, hotels, and shops. And to Buford's pockets, of course. He left that part out. Detailing the legitimacy of the business proved a little more difficult. No way was he going to part with trade secrets like fungus mixed with ley lines. Hell, everyone knew bizarre things happened in Silverville, so why did they even ask? Several from the Commission even insisted on complimentary Day Trips. In the end, he offered a compromise, a single free pass. Whoever ended up time-traveling would have to report the experience to the others.

Ka Catchers also attracted the attention of Brother Martin's crazy congregation, The Church of the Holy Grail. A few years back, they'd gotten all excited about Howard's UFO sighting, believing the "Mother Ship" had come to take them home. They'd continued to show their craziness when Buford left the commissioners' meeting about The Time Portal. Martin and his followers were marching around the courthouse with placards stating, "God hates time travel" and "God condemns Buford Price." One idiot, who obviously called in sick one too many school days, held a sign that said, "Get a brain, Moreon!"

As soon as Buford walked down the building's stone steps, the whole group swarmed around him, flinging insults, but nothing else. Probably because the county sheriff, Carl, leaned on a patrol car parked nearby. Buford puffed out his chest and made a beeline toward one of the protesters.

"And when did you last talk to God?" he demanded. "You're part of His inner circle of friends? Did He tell you to wear that ridiculous toupee?"

The man shrank away. "B-but this is my real hair."

"And you!" Buford thundered, pointing to the man holding the *Moreon* sign. "God hates bad spellers!"

The crowd parted, allowing their victim to pass unharmed.

No, Micah needn't worry about any little speed bumps. In the end, Buford would work them all out.

As the plane descended, the scenery disappeared in a thick cloud of ground fog. Buford heard the clunk of landing gear and unbuckled his seatbelt early. The woman sitting in the next seat looked at him and scowled. Big deal. They'd land in only a few minutes.

He started to return the scowl, but instead felt the unexpected and powerful wallop of the plane hitting the runway. The hard landing threw him straight upward, his head colliding with the "fasten seatbelts" sign and cracking the console. At the same time, the doors to the overhead bins bounced open and carry-on luggage flew into the aisle. An audible gasp sounded throughout the cabin. A few people screamed and swore.

"Welcome to Denver International Airport," the captain crooned over the intercom. "Thank you for flying with us today. Please remain seated and keep your seatbelts fastened until the plane comes to a complete stop."

Buford reached to the top of his head and fingered a lump that seemed to swell with each passing second. Smug and righteous, his seatmate handed him a napkin to swab the blood trickling down his temple.

"What happened to that man?" a child across the aisle asked, pointing in Buford's direction.

The annoying woman snapped a response: "He can't follow rules."

APRIL accompanied Micah and Mr. Smith as far as the flashy façade hiding the outhouse. Along the way, the Ka Catcher team stressed the importance of focusing on the time and place once inside The Time Portal.

"It's sort of like what Dorothy did when she clicked her heels together three times," Micah said. "'There's no place like home. There's no place like home.' And that's where she ended up."

"What?" Mr. Smith asked. "Who is this Dorothy?"

"Never mind," April said. "You just think about southern Turkey and goat herding twelve-thousand years ago."

Micah unlocked the façade door, and he and Mr. Smith entered.

"Bon voyage, Mr. Smith," April called out. "Have a good trip."

She waited outside but heard him gasp and say, "Is this some sort of joke?" Yep, Micah must be leading him into the outhouse.

After a few minutes, Micah joined her.

"He's on his way," he said.

"How long before I can go on my own Day Trip?" She'd decided her destination would be Tintagel Castle in fifth-century Cornwall, England. She didn't expect to find the Round Table or Holy Grail, but she wanted to see if there really was a King Arthur and Merlin.

"Beats me. Now's as good a time as any, I guess."

They entered through the façade, but Micah stopped at the outhouse door. "You're on your own from here."

April took a deep breath and approached the door.

"Wait!" Micah reached out, touching her arm. "Maybe you should take out your contacts first. Gonna be in there for a while."

She popped out the designer star lenses, placed them in a small carrying case, and dropped it in her pocket.

Giving him a hug, she stepped inside the outhouse.

APRIL barely had time to notice Mr. Smith slumped against the wall, or the sign on the inside door, reading, "This Way Out," before she found herself curled up next to a rock on a grassy hill.

The first sound she heard was the nearby bleating of goats.

Still a little disoriented, she stood and turned in circles for signs of a castle. But as far as she could see there was nothing but rolling hills dotted with grazing goats. She trotted up a knoll to get a better of idea of how close she was to the coast of the Celtic Sea.

No water in sight.

"Shit!"

She looked down at her clothing. Clearly a man's, but instead of the fifth-century linen or woolen garb she expected, her clothing more resembled a shift dress of crude animal skins. This didn't look like Arthur's Cornwall, or even Dorothy's Kansas.

Her destination looked a lot more like southern Turkey twelve-thousand years ago.

But if that were so, where was Mr. Smith?

From her knoll, she saw a disturbance in the herd. All the animals moved away from one particular goat, which looked at her and started bleating.

"Uh-oh."

The unpopular goat started up the knoll, running toward her. At the moment it rounded a craggy outcropping, a large spotted leopard leaped from one of the rocks and took down the goat with a single swipe.

She watched in horror as the cat settled over the carcass to devour its prey.

BUFORD shuffled along with the herd of deplaning passengers. Most people pulled out cell phones as they walked up the stairs and into the spacious main hallway of Concourse B. Might as well use his own cell like everyone else and check in with Ka Catchers.

He pressed the speed dial key and waited for an answer, but only April's recorded voice greeted him. "Welcome to Ka Catchers! Isn't it *time* to take time into your own hands? We're unable to answer your –" He snapped the phone shut. Damn kids, what the hell were they doing that was so important they couldn't take calls?

Straight ahead he funneled into a crowd of people queuing to step onto the first section of moving sidewalks running the length of the concourse. "Mind your step," the automated voice warned. Buford didn't, pitching forward into the folks directly in front of him. The domino effect jostled a cluster of travelers, who gripped the side rails to keep from falling. All turned and glared his way. He twisted to the man behind him, trying to pass off the faux pas, and scolded in a loud voice, "Hey, pal, watch out!"

The sidewalk whisked him along to the entrance of the underground trains that would take him to the main terminal. Once he reached the center of the concourse, he stepped onto stationary flooring, headed down a flight of stairs, and elbowed his way to the train. He dropped his duffel bag on a seat and plopped down before an old lady with a walker could reach the bench. It was a short ride; she'd be okay.

The train finally arrived at its destination and pulled to a stop. The passengers stampeded to the doors, jostling and pushing one another. The old lady who'd wanted his seat seemed to make a point of rolling her walker over his foot. He hated cities and mindless crowds who moved like flocks of sheep. He'd be glad to get back to Silverville.

Too bad his dealings with the limo company would keep him in Denver overnight. They'd promised they could close the deal and detail the car he selected by the first thing next morning. In the meantime, he would look over their fleet, but he already knew the one he wanted: a 2012 six-passenger Lincoln. Pearl white with two-tone black leather seats and a small bar.

His ride came to a stop and he stepped off the train at the main terminal. Making his way past incoming passengers, he walked outside and hailed a cab to take him to the dealership.

MICAH sat in a folding chair situated just outside the outhouse. He unscrewed his thermos and took a swig of coffee to wash down the donut. He figured this part of his job would be the most boring. The waiting. At least he'd remembered to bring a book.

He still worried about two people taking Day Trips at the same time. Initially, Buford had proposed offering multiple-party trips, but he and April had talked him out of it. They certainly hadn't worked through the consequences, and here they were, trying it on the spur of the moment anyway. He thought back to April's argument about her own trip. *What could go wrong?* Chances were, nothing, but it still made him uncomfortable.

He sure wouldn't want anything bad to happen to her. Yeah, she was bossy, but easier to talk to than Sarah. April had even stood up for him when Buford had tried to short them on pay. Sarah hadn't defended him when her father marched him to the stocks. And April sure looked great in that Cleopatra outfit – a real improvement over a gray Puritan dress and bonnet.

April was beautiful, confident, clever – and she lived in the twenty-first century. Of course, she wore lizard lenses and lied for effect. He'd never met anybody so eccentric, but that made her all the more interesting. And despite their rocky introduction, they'd become comrades-in-arms against a world created by Buford Price. Micah even found himself imagining the two of them as a couple.

He laughed out loud. No girl had ever liked spending time with him. Still, was it possible she might one day see more in him than just a coworker? Only one way to find out: He'd take the plunge, invite her to a movie or out to coffee.

Pushing into the chair to find a more comfortable position, he leaned back and daydreamed about a future with someone as complicated as April.

An hour later, the outhouse door blew open and the woman of his dreams stumbled out.

"Micah!" she gasped.

"That was quick." He moved over to help steady her. "How come you're back so soon?"

Breathing hard, she rasped, "Mr. Smith ..."

"He back already, too?" He looked toward the outhouse.

"That's what I'm trying to tell you. Mr. Smith isn't coming back."

BUFORD settled into the back seat of the taxi as the cab exited the DIA complex. According to the driver, the trip would take thirty-five minutes to reach downtown Denver and another fifteen to the parking lot of Captain Clark's Preferred Luxury Limousines.

Popping open his satchel, Buford removed several photos he'd printed from the Internet describing the Lincoln MKS he'd inquired about two days earlier. Even with 36,000 miles, the vehicle still had a sticker price he could meet only by adding a second mortgage to Price's Gun Paradise. An all-wheel-drive stretch, powered by a V-6, 3.6 litre engine, seating six passengers comfortably. The limo came fully stocked with two flat screen TVs, DVD player, beverage bars, surround sound, and LED interior lights. The pearl exterior contrasted tastefully with the plush champagne interior.

"You might consider a deposit to hold it," Captain Clark advised over the phone. "I've got someone else coming to look at it in the morning."

But Buford knew the man was lying, a ploy to rush the sale.

Once he struck the deal, he'd own the only limousine in Silverville. When the business didn't need the car for ghost tours, he would drive it around himself to advertise. Folks would turn and stare at his new wheels, nodding knowingly that Buford Price was the big man in town. Plus it would be a great babe magnet. Lots of room in the back seats to entertain the ladies. Stretch out and … whatever.

As the cab merged onto I-70, a sleek black limo passed them westbound into Denver. Dark-tinted windows prevented him from seeing the passengers, but he got a clear view of the driver wearing a smart chauffeur's cap. Yes, that was something he'd have to get for Perry. One thing Buford knew for sure – image was everything.

He caught sight of himself in the cabbie's rearview mirror; dried blood painted unnatural bangs across his forehead. Damn, he'd forgotten about his little incident when the plane touched down. He fished a comb from his pocket and tried to smooth his hair. Next he spat onto his handkerchief and rubbed it over the blood. His eyes met the cabbie's, also looking in the mirror.

"Hey, man, you okay?" the driver asked. "Need me to take you to the hospital?"

"No, no." Buford laughed. "Bit of a mishap on the plane. Lucky for everyone else I was there to help."

The cabbie shrugged. "Suit yourself."

Twenty minutes later, they pulled into the dealership, which sprawled across half a city block. Buford stepped out of the cab, paid the driver, and scanned the lot until he spotted the Lincoln MKS parked outside the showroom. The sun glinted off the metallic pearl finish, and he knew immediately he'd made the right choice. Strutting over to the driver window, he peered inside at the leather seats.

That's when he noticed the "sold" sign pasted over the price sheet. A bit presumptuous to assume he'd take the limo before looking it over. And he didn't plan to pay full mark-up.

"A beauty, isn't she?"

Buford twirled around to see a tall, white-haired gentleman wearing an expensive white suit, white shirt and white tie. The only color was a pale blue carnation attached to his lapel. The man thrust out a hand. "Captain Clark."

Buford peeled the soggy, stained handkerchief off his palm and reached out to shake. "Buford Price. From Silverville. We spoke yesterday, and I'm glad to see you saved this vehicle for me."

A look of confusion flashed across Clark's face. "There must be some mistake. I just sold this limo to the Governor's Office."

"What the hell? I thought we had a deal."

Captain Clark looked him up and down for a moment. "No, we had a conversation. I believe I mentioned we had another interested party."

Buford whined, "So you sold it out from under me?"

"We had no specific deal, Mr. Price." He paused. "But I have something else that might fit your needs."

Buford glanced at the line-up of other vehicles – a Cadillac Escalade, a stretched Hummer, and scores of other limos longer than his house – all of them tricked out to carry a dozen or more passengers. "None of these will work. Too big."

"I didn't mean one of these." Captain Clark took him by the elbow. "Come with me."

Clark led him behind the showroom toward a large garage. "Tell me again what sort of business you're starting over in Leadville."

"Silverville," Buford corrected.

"Oh yeah. Right. That's where all the UFO craze is."

Buford puffed up. "That was all my doing. Put our little burg on the map. But my latest enterprise is gonna knock everybody's socks off. We've engineered a time portal to the past."

"Uh-huh." The dealer flicked on a panel of lights, illuminating the space with an eerie green glow. "Some sort of virtual reality theme park?"

"Nothing of the sort. We're talking about the real deal."

But Buford lost his train of thought when he realized what had cast the greenish glow in the garage. The bright fluorescent lights overhead reflected against the garish paint of a vehicle dominating the center of the building.

"Kind of takes your breath away, doesn't it?"

Buford could agree with that. He felt the man propel him toward the monstrosity.

"One owner. Less mileage than the Lincoln – only 28,000," Clark said. "A custom-built Chrysler 300 limousine." He ran his hand over the hood until he reached and opened the driver door. "Come on, now, it's not going to bite."

"But the color," Buford gasped.

"We call it neon chartreuse." Without missing a beat, he continued, "This baby sports matching interior, soft white vinyl top, tinted windows, custom bar, star lights, fiber optic lights, privacy divider window, rear AM/FM stereo with CD player, DVD player, flat screen TV, dual batteries, dual alternators, heavy-duty suspension, rear air and heat." He took a breath. "Plus custom 20-inch chrome wheels."

"But the color…"

"Truly one of a kind. You'll never see another one like it. Can't you see yourself owning this fine luxury limousine?"

"When pigs fly," Buford muttered.

"And you know the best thing about this vehicle?"

"What?"

"Only twenty-two grand. A far cry from the seventy-five on that Lincoln."

At this, Buford perked up. He opened the rear passenger door and poked his head inside. "How many does it seat?"

"Much roomier. This one holds ten."

Buford started mentally calculating. At twenty-two grand, maybe he wouldn't need as big a second mortgage. And the extra seating capacity could allow him to pile more customers into the back. Hell, it didn't have to be just the families of Day Trippers who got to use it. He'd open up the ghost tours to anybody who came to town for whatever reason.

But that color – it reminded him of something. He studied the long green panel separating the front from the rear wheels. "Reminds me of the pea-green puke from the movie, *The Exorcist*."

"Or the ectoplasm in *Ghostbusters*. Didn't you say you planned to use it for ghost tours?"

Oh, yeah, ectoplasm. He snapped his fingers. Ectoplasm! Perfect. It might just work after all. He could call it the Ectomobile.

"Would you take twenty?"

"We might be able to work with that sum."

"And you'd need to detail the car and throw in a tank of gas."

"Certainly. If you'd take it off our – er, I mean, if we can have the pleasure of seeing you drive it off the lot. We could have it ready for you first thing tomorrow morning."

Buford took Captain Clark by the elbow this time. "Let's go sign the papers."

AT FIRST, they debated what could have gone wrong – besides the fact a leopard had eaten their first client. Why hadn't April gone to her own destination? They decided the only explanation was that April had ridden Smith's coattails to ancient Turkey. Now they knew The Time Portal could only open into one place at a time. And evidently, in the case of two simultaneous travelers, the portal closed when one of the Day Trips ended. At least that's what happened to April: Smith's Ka died and hers shot back to the outhouse.

Now they had an even bigger problem on their hands.

Micah held a donut to the man's lips. "Eat!"

Mr. Smith's mouth opened and took a bite. Micah looked at April. "See, he's eating."

"Yeah, but it's not really him."

Earlier that morning, Smith had wandered from the outhouse door not long after April came back. But something wasn't right. He didn't fully wake up, and he couldn't seem to speak except for noises that sounded kind of like bleats.

"He's not in there," April had said, waving her hands in front of the man's face. "His Ba isn't coming back. His personality died when the leopard ate the body he occupied."

"So, what have we got here?" Micah asked.

"Looks like he still has a functioning body."

101

Mr. Smith bleated and looked at the donut in Micah's hand. He gave him another bite.

"Let's see what else he can do," April suggested.

They led the zombie to the work shed behind the ranch house, and she offered him a rake. His hands grasped the tool, but otherwise he stood motionless.

"Rake!" April commanded.

The man raked.

"Stop raking and put the tool back."

He did so.

"Okay," April said, "There's still enough brain function that he takes simple orders."

Micah stared at Mr. Smith for a couple of minutes. He swallowed hard. "We're in a heap of trouble. We'll have to hide him."

April let her eyes turn toward the driveway. "And we've got to get rid of that car."

"Oh shit! The car." Micah dropped the partially eaten donut and looked like he might throw up. "What're we gonna do?"

"Let's check it out."

She took Micah by one hand and Mr. Smith by the other and led them over to the Honda. Mr. Smith showed no recognition at all.

"Would he own a car like this?" Micah asked.

"Not likely. Bet it's a rental to go along with the rest of his disguise."

She circled the vehicle, looking for a sticker or any identifying signage. Nothing. She tried the door. Unlocked. She slid into the passenger seat and popped the glove box. A folded car rental agreement spilled out. Scanning the contents, April saw it originated from a Denver company, but the name on the contract wasn't Mr. Smith. It was Mr. Jones. Looked like he tried to hide his identity from Rentals-R-Us, just like he'd tried to hide it from

Ka Catchers. She doubted anyone would find a Mr. Jones or a Mr. Smith from the Republic of Yadim.

"We're in luck." She reached over and snatched up the keys lying in the driver's seat. "There's a Rentals-R-Us here at the airport. You're going to drive it over there, leave it in the parking lot, and drop the paperwork and keys in the drop box. In a couple days, this car will be in Utah or Nevada."

He nodded but glanced over at Smith. "But we're still stuck with him. What are we going to do with Mr. Zombie here? We still need to hide him, too."

"Not necessarily. I've got an idea." She peeled off his Rolex and expensive rings, and stuffed them in her pocket.

Micah scowled.

"I'm not stealing," she explained. "We need to hide these, too, so no one recognizes his flashy jewelry."

April picked up the donut, brushed off the gravel, and led Mr. Smith inside the barn. She tore off a chunk of pastry and tossed it to the ground. Their new zombie dropped to his hands and knees and scrambled to get it. She tore up the rest and scattered it across the barn floor.

"There. That oughta keep him busy for a while." She pushed Micah outside, shutting and locking the door behind her. "I'll pick you up at the airport soon as I run another errand."

She threw him the Honda's keys and started for her own car.

Micah took her arm and stopped her. "How are we going to explain this to Buford?"

"We won't. We'll tell him we hired a fill-in for Howard when he's at his other job."

"That won't work. Buford's met him, and he knows what he looks like."

"Not when I'm done with him." She winked and turned away, calling over her shoulder. "Meet you in twenty minutes."

103

BUFORD breathed a sigh, relieved the Denver traffic had begun to thin the further he traveled westward from the city. Driving a vehicle this long was no easy task. Soon after he pulled out of the dealer parking lot, he'd thumped over several corner curbs and nearly run over a woman waiting at a bus stop.

He also figured out the time needed to bring the limo to a stop was much longer than a regular car. Driving through downtown, a rude SUV had darted in front of him just as the two approached a light turning red. Buford had stomped on the brakes, barely avoiding a rear-end collision. Infuriated, he pounded the car horn, only to hear an abbreviated harmonica rendition of the William Tell Overture. Not quite believing his ears, he pounded again. That *was* the horn. No one at the dealership had mentioned that custom feature. The guy who'd cut him off leaned out his window and looked back at the Ectomobile with Lone Ranger sound effects. Then he

flipped Buford the bird.

After that, Buford took extra care to baby his new wheels. Despite the color, the Ectomobile had a flawless exterior and an immaculate interior. He caressed the supple leather seat, marveling at its pristine condition. He intended to keep it that way. But he might change the horn when he got home.

Forty miles out of town, the road changed to single lanes and started the ascent toward the Continental Divide. The number of cars on the highway diminished, replaced by a growing population of pickup trucks and campers. No chance he was going to pass one of them with all the twisting turns and yellow lines. Mountain driving was always a trade-off – fewer cars but more chance of getting stuck behind a slowpoke.

He spotted a convenience store along the road and pulled in to get a cup of coffee. Once inside, he noticed the clerk standing at the window staring at the limo. He turned to Buford.

"There's the most god awful green buggy parked out there."

"Yeah, but I bet it's really decked out inside." Buford padded over to the coffee machine and poured himself a tall one. That should keep him alert for the three hours ahead.

Besides the clerk, Buford was the only other person inside the store.

The clerk must have noticed it, too. "Hey, man, that limo isn't yours, is it?" Buford didn't have a chance to respond. The clerk waved away the money. "On the house. Sorry 'bout what I said."

"Laugh all you want. I'll be making a bundle with this 'buggy,' and you'll still be working in this convenience store."

"In that case, that'll be a buck fifty."

Buford tossed two dollars on the counter and stormed out the door.

He slid into the Ectomobile, placed his coffee in the cup holder, and backed out of the parking spot to get onto the highway. Before he could maneuver onto the highway, a truck pulling a livestock trailer rumbled by, only inches from his front bumper. Even through rolled up windows, Buford caught the unmistakable stench of pigs. At least it wasn't a logging truck. He'd heard stories of logs breaking free and slamming into the cars behind. He'd nevertheless keep a wide berth so no pig shit hit his windshield.

He drove onto the road and settled in behind the trailer, making sure to keep at least four or five car lengths away. He sipped his coffee. Tomorrow about this time, their first paying customer, Mr. Smith, would begin his Day Trip. The man reeked of power – not to mention that entourage of bodyguards kowtowing to his every whim. He'd probably pick a Day Trip that let him hobnob with power brokers from the past. Buford could see him astride a Roman charger, leading legions down a cobbled street and a victory garland perched on his head. Or maybe a

Viking earl, sloshing mead over a table, blonde Nordic beauties swooning at his feet. Yeah, that's the sort of trip he'd take.

But he didn't care what Mr. Smith's Day Trip was, just so long as it was good enough to recommend Ka Catchers to all his cronies. That'd clinch his reputation, and Buford would raise the price to cater to the rich and famous – politicians, CEOs, and the like. Top drawer all the way.

Buford realized he'd pressed the accelerator too hard in his excitement over his first client, and the limo had edged up too close to the pigs ahead. He coasted until he paced behind the livestock load from a safer distance.

The road straightened out a bit, and he saw a chance to get around the annoying aroma of swine piping through the dashboard vents. He tromped on the gas pedal. The extra weight of the Chrysler took forever to build up enough momentum to pass.

Good thing he had a straight stretch of road since the trickiest climb was only a couple miles ahead, the hairpin turns of Mule Ear Pass.

Up ahead stood a sign to watch for falling rocks. He'd never paid much attention to these warnings because what could you do to stop a falling rock? He laughed at the thought as he leaned into the first curve. With only a half second to react, he saw a basketball-sized boulder resting in the middle of the highway. Buford cut a tight swerve into the oncoming lane, barely missing the rock. Lucky for him, no one was on that side of the road. Unlucky for the Ectomobile was the half cup of coffee that sloshed from the holder and onto passenger seat and down to the plush knap of the floorboard carpeting.

He swore and patted his jacket pockets for a napkin or handkerchief – anything to mop up the coffee. All he found was the dealership paperwork, but that would do. He reached across the center console, dabbing at the brown mess. He turned his eyes back to the road in time to see a large bull elk sauntering across his path from the left.

Buford jerked the wheel to the right, missing by inches the rock wall that bordered the inside lane. He felt the remainder of the coffee searing his leg and running into his sock.

"Goddamn son-of-a-bitch!" he gasped.

He couldn't pull off until he reached a scenic overlook at the pass's summit, where he stepped out of the limo and inspected it for damage. No dings or scratches, just a little dust. He leaned against the driver door to slow his heart and catch his breath. *Leapin' Jesus, I was lucky.* Could have been bad, real bad. Why the hell couldn't the state fence off these roads to keep elk from sabotaging motorists?

He heard the whine of an overworked engine on the switchback below and caught sight of the pig truck chugging up the mountain. No way did he want to get behind that thing again. He jumped into the front seat, started the Chrysler, and pulled back onto the road. He dropped the transmission into second gear and hovered his foot over the brake pedal as he descended the even steeper western slope of the pass.

It took the next three sharp corners to adjust his speed, taking care not to clip the side of his limo on rocks jutting above the narrow shoulder. A green sign at the side of the road told him Silverville lay only fifty-four miles away. Buford allowed his fingers to relax and his fleshy lips blew a relieved breath. He let his shoulders drop and settled back into the leather seat. Tapping the radio switch, he searched for easy-listening music to match his lightening mood. He was home free.

He thought.

It happened so fast. First the thud on the hood, then the crash through the windshield that left him nose to nose with a small black pig. He heard screaming and squealing but couldn't tell if it came from him or his new passenger. It struggled to free itself from the broken glass, legs striking and tangling the spokes of the steering wheel. He craned from left to right to see past the pig and find a safe place to stop; all the while the animal's snout snapped at Buford's face as he dodged to avoid getting bitten.

He couldn't tell where his car came to a stop, but he lunged out the door. Now he could see the predicament. A small pig had lodged firmly into his windshield – the front half flailing over the steering wheel, and the back half floundering and scratching the hood. He placed tentative hands on each back leg and yanked. The animal wouldn't budge, but it screamed louder with each of Buford's tugs.

Retreating a step or two, he wondered if a rock would break the rest of the windshield and he could free the pig. He retrieved a hefty, jagged piece of granite lying next to the shoulder and climbed onto the hood, slamming the rock into the glass next to the squealing animal. A few cracks spiderwebbed from the point of impact, but the shield remained intact. He continued to pound, shouting, "Can't be happening! Can't be happening!" with each strike.

"Move your vehicle to the shoulder, and then remain in your seat," a loud speaker commanded.

Buford paused from pounding and looked up to see a highway patrol car parked behind him. "But the pig will bite me."

"Move your vehicle to the shoulder, and remain in your seat," the loud speaker repeated.

Buford climbed off the hood and crawled into the front seat, ducking the gnashing teeth while he complied with the order. He rolled down his window and saw a state trooper standing slightly behind the door.

"Got a little problem?" a woman's voice asked.

Buford twisted in his seat to see the officer, swatting at the pig. "Can I get out?"

Her eyes traveled from Buford to the squirming beast and back to Buford. "Is this your pig, sir?"

"Well, no, it came out of nowhere," Buford shouted over the squealing.

"We have laws in this state against animal cruelty."

"But it flew into my windshield."

She paused. "Are you saying this is a *flying* pig?"

"Look, lady, I need to get out of the car."

"You can call me Officer Aboc, and I pulled you over for obstructing the highway." She stepped back and motioned to him. "Okay, step out. Keep your hands where I can see them."

Buford scrunched down and rolled out of the seat, tumbling onto the asphalt. He peered up at the trooper. Her hand rested on the holster of a big gun, watching him warily. When he stood, he found the woman to be much shorter than he, but she looked all business. Stray wisps of blond hair snapped in the breeze against the brim of her Smokey-the-Bear hat. But he couldn't see her eyes behind the dark-tinted sunshades.

"License and registration, please."

He fumbled out his wallet to hand her the license. "I don't have a registration. I just bought this vehicle."

"Then I'll need to see your paperwork."

Those papers were now in a soggy brown puddle on the front seat. "Okay, but you have to distract the pig."

"Stay here," she said. "I might have something in my lunch pail."

The trooper took a long time in her car, undoubtedly verifying his driver's license and looking for farmyard food. When she returned, Trooper Aboc handed him his license and held out an apple to the pig. "Get the paperwork."

While Buford scurried to the passenger side of the limo, she cooed at the pig and stroked its head while it munched on the apple. Buford gathered the dripping wad of dealership papers and walked to her side of the limo to hand them over.

"Sort of hard to read but they look legit." She held the documents up to the sun and then looked at him. "Sir, I'm going to have to cite you for ... Well, I'm not exactly sure what."

The trooper's radio squawked and she walked back to her car. A few moments later, she came back and said, "I'm letting you off this time because I have an emergency halfway down this side of the pass. Have a nice day."

"Wait! Aren't you going to help me with this pig?"

"Not today, Mr. Price. I've got a whole overturned trailer of scattered pigs to deal with right now."

She tipped her hat and hurried back to her car. He watched her U-turn and speed away.

Buford peered inside the Ectomobile. His uninvited traveling companion looked content and appeared to be sleeping, which gave him a chance to ease inside. Maybe he could get back to Silverville before it woke up. He'd have Howard and Micah figure out how to extract the animal.

He started the Chrysler but left off his seatbelt so he could lean in either direction to see the road. Between the snoring and apple juice saliva, it would be a long fifty-four miles home.

CHAPTER SIX

"It's adorable!" April said. She dabbed antiseptic ointment on the pig's neck.

"Yeah, in a grunting, rooting sort of way." Micah squatted down to pet the new arrival, too.

She stroked the wiry hairs springing from the little porcine shoulders, realizing she'd never been this close to any kind of swine before – well, not outside the sliced and stacked tenderloins and cutlets at the grocery store meat counter. She'd seen the occasional one at a distance on this and that ranch, of course, on trips out of town. But they never seemed to be in petting zoos. That made no sense, she thought, as the pig pushed hard into her caress.

"No way we're keeping it," insisted Buford.

"I'm naming it Breakfast," April said.

"I'll go find a bowl." Micah stood and called over his shoulder as he headed toward the Welcome Center. "What do pigs eat anyway?"

"Hands, fingers," Buford muttered.

"For Pete's sake, Buford." April scowled at him. "It's an injured animal. We have to take care of it."

She and Micah had listened to him tell the story while they gently extracted the pig from the windshield. Flying pig? No. This poor little thing apparently tumbled from the overturned livestock trailer on the switchback above Buford.

"How'd you even see through the windshield driving home? And why didn't you take it out?"

"No easy task, cars honking at me 'cause all they could see was a pig's ass stuck in glass coming head on. It was just too ferocious to remove."

Breakfast rolled over for a pat on the belly. "I wonder if it's a boy or a girl?"

Micah returned with a bowl filled with chopped apples and carrots. "Duh, it doesn't have a, a –"

"Wee-wee?" April suggested.

Micah's face reddened.

Buford walked over to the limo and flicked a finger at a dry pig turd hanging from the grill. "Look at this poor new car."

"Yeah, look at it," Micah replied. "Was this the only color they had?"

"I asked for it. Matches the theme of our ghost tours. We'll call it the Ectomobile."

April started to laugh. "Or the Snotmobile."

While they discussed the dismal condition of Buford's new purchase, Howard pedaled up the driveway. He laid his bike on the grass, trotted over to the limo, and ran his fingers across the long row of windows on the side. He turned to Buford with a wide grin. "This your new car, Mr. Price?"

"Yeah, and your job is to wash it."

"It's the most beautiful car I've ever seen!"

Buford faced Micah. "And your job is to take it to the garage tomorrow for a new windshield." He glared at April and Breakfast. "Make sure you get that pig outta here before Mr. Smith arrives in the morning."

Oh God, here it comes. She hoped Micah could stick to their devious plan and flat out lie to Buford. "About that... Mr. Smith won't be coming tomorrow. He's postponed indefinitely."

"I hope he doesn't expect a refund!"

Micah mumbled to April, "No worries about that."

"This business has a no-return policy. You told him about that, didn't you? We haven't had any more confirmed reservations as it is. You two need to get out there and promote more Day Trips." He pointed an accusing finger directly at April. "Shouldn't you be getting ready for that travel show?"

With the catastrophe of Mr. Smith's return, April had forgotten she had her first promotional junket that weekend at the Denver Trade Center. They'd booked a booth in the Exhibition Hall at the last minute for some big vacation and adventure expo. Travel companies from across the country would be there, but no one would offer anything as exotic as Ka Catchers.

Still jabbing his finger at the air in front of April's nose, Buford continued, "Summer's half gone, and we need lots of bookings if this business is going to ..." Buford paused, his eyes looking past April. "Who the hell's that?"

She swiveled on the ground beside the pig and watched their only client shuffle out of the barn, still hugging the empty box of caramel corn he'd eaten two hours ago. In no way did he resemble the original Mr. Smith Buford had met. The orange hair dye and oversize reading glasses helped take care of that. No longer a man of the world, this Mr. Smith could barely find his way out of the barn.

"That's Howard's new friend," she said, glancing at Micah to jump in any time.

"It is?" Howard beamed.

"Yes," Micah added. "Don't you remember you brought him here to help out?"

"I did?"

"Great, another slacker on the payroll," Buford grumbled.

April stopped scratching Breakfast's belly and stood. "Don't have to pay him. He'll work for food."

Buford shifted weight from one leg to the other, scrutinizing his new employee who now upended the empty box over his mouth, murmuring, "Mm, mm."

"You sure he can work?"

"Absolutely. He raked all the leaves off the yard just this morning." *Well, eventually he might.*

"So, what's his name?"

Micah shot her an uncomfortable glance.

Oh shit, we didn't discuss that. She bit her lip, looking at Mr. Smith and his hollow box of …

"It's, uh, Cracker Jack."

APRIL lugged the duffel bag over to the row of exhibition registration windows filling the back wall inside the Pavilion welcome center. For an early Saturday morning, the queues seemed disturbingly long. Above each ticket window ran a display of different ranges of alphabetical letters – A-C, D-F, all the way to Z. Kind of reminded her of the mega theater chains that funneled people into neat little categories to buy tickets for the assorted blockbuster flavors of the week. If only Silverville still had a movie house! She'd heard the town's only theater had closed several years before, the space now occupied by a local crackpot group called The Church of the Holy Grail. She'd have to check that out some time – once she and Micah had worked out their rotation for keeping an eye on Cracker Jack.

To her left, she noticed a much shorter line with a sign reading "Exhibitor Check In." Even shorter lines stood in front of windows for each featured event. Relieved she wouldn't have to carry her load much further, she walked over and got in the queue for the travel show. She'd gotten lost on all the one-way streets in downtown Denver, once spotting the Pavilion Hall a block away but perplexed at how to get there. In the end, she'd parked a half mile away, resigned to the reality of arriving late.

When her turn at the window arrived, a woman at the counter smiled, but with no warmth on her face. The gaze fell to a computer screen. "Name?"

"April Schauers."

The woman tapped at her keyboard several times and frowned. "I don't see that registration."

April suggested she try Buford Price, but the worker gave her the same frown. Ka Catchers? Nope, nothing for that entry either.

Great. Buford's parting words early that morning clanged in her head. *Everything's arranged, so make us proud!* Right, if she could get in the door. But what did he say last weekend when he made the last-minute reservations? Something about being "short-listed" for space but a promise they'd get a slot *somewhere*.

She rapped on the counter to get the registration worker's attention. "Do you have other shows here this weekend?"

The roll of the woman's eyes said, *Duh!*

"Were we maybe booked into another show by mistake?" April fluttered her eyelids innocently.

A deeper frown – probably part concentration and part offense at April's impudence – furrowed Miss Sunshine's face as she tapped more keys and scrutinized the screen. "Oh, here it is." She flashed a withering look over the counter as if to imply the misfiling was April's fault. The printer behind the counter whirred and the woman reached down to tear off an exhibitor's badge, which she slipped into a lanyard and handed to April. "Up the stairs and at the end of the corridor."

"But which show is it?"

"Can't miss it. There's a giant faucet on display just outside."

"But – "

"Next!"

April backed away, slipping the lanyard over her head, and heaved the duffel to her shoulder. She trundled up the stairs and past the travel exhibition entrance, peering inside as she walked by. That travel show was huge, lined with rows of tables and displays stretching deeper than a field goal kick. Maybe just as well she couldn't set up shop inside. Her meager little displays would pale among all the towering promotionals she glimpsed as she continued down the corridor.

Up ahead, a cluster of people gawked at a huge shiny faucet perched above the final door in the complex. Children pointed and giggled while adults snapped pictures before going through the entrance. April stopped short.

The placard on the lintel over the door read, "Bed, Bath, and Kitchen Extravaganza."

Fifteen minutes later, April found her table squeezed between a rack of deep plush towels on one side and a much larger arrangement of bathtubs on the other. Shrugging off her duffel, she pulled out the banner and taped it onto the front of her six-foot-wide table. Next, she pulled out their shiny new brochures, filled with glossy prints from the commercial they'd shot a few weeks earlier. Her favorite was still Buford, half unseated by his steed. But the waving arm in the still looked valiant even though she knew he was struggling to retrieve one flapping rein.

Extravaganza customers had already begun to mill and wander the aisles when she set up her laptop with a slideshow of exotic pictures portraying the past. Her table looked sparse compared to the dazzling fixtures and appliances facing her on the other side of the aisle, and she noticed a rather dour woman staring at her from the Towels-R-Us booth to the side.

Oh! The lizard lenses, she thought. Maybe better to go with something a bit more demure for this crowd. April rummaged in the duffel bag's side pouch, where she'd stashed her spares. Maybe lavender and sparkles would set the proper tone. The lenses certainly complemented the nearest porcelain bathtub on her other side.

She just had time to make the switch when the first browsers sauntered by.

"U THER YET?" Micah thumbed onto the keypad of his new phone.

One of the better perks of his new job was the smart phones he and April had finagled out of Buford – a begrudging concession on his part, for sure. But April had insisted they all needed to coordinate their activities and stay in touch. Their employer grumbled about the expense, especially since phone reception seemed limited to Silverville and the immediate environs. In fact, even Ka Catchers had a spotty signal.

His phone vibrated and April's reply appeared on the phone. "Y/N."

"Looks like she made it – sort of," Micah called out to Buford, who was taping a poster of Medieval Europe on the wall.

Right behind Buford stood the pig, who'd developed an unexpected attachment to the man. She followed him everywhere, hovering at his feet – and sometimes underfoot.

Micah couldn't resist setting up what happened next.

"See for yourself," he said, holding out his phone.

Buford looked over his shoulder at Micah and turned to step closer to read the message. And fell over Breakfast's low center of mass, sending him sprawling to the floor.

Buford picked himself up, scowling at the pig. "Damn it! We've got to do something about that, that ..." He thrust open hands toward the animal, scowling as it snorted and waddled over to lean into his leg.

Breakfast had already earned her keep, so far as Micah was concerned. Buford seemed too distracted to ask him any more questions about "Cracker Jack," which suited Micah just fine.

He'd been nervous about April leaving him alone so soon after the fiasco with their first Day Tripper.

Micah shoved the phone toward Buford, who read the cryptic message.

"What's that mean?"

"Yes and no. Must be having some problems."

Buford bent down to shove the pig away. "Well, find out what's going on."

"I'll ask her." Micah tapped into his phone, "sup?" *What's going on?*

"l8ter," came the reply.

"She'll get back to us later. Sounds like she's busy."

"She better be." Buford stormed out of the Welcome Center but didn't close the door in time to stop Breakfast from trailing along behind.

A WOMAN with three little kids in tow paused at April's table and picked up a brochure, puzzling over the pictures. The smallest child tugged at her mother's pant leg and whispered loudly, "That lady has pink eye."

The woman glanced up at April, a look of horror widening her eyes. She threw the brochure on the floor and stared at her hands. "Don't touch anything!"

She backed away as April tried to explain. "No, my eyes are lavender. And they're just – "

But the woman herded her children away with her elbows, shouting, "Where's the restroom?"

Sheesh, what's up with her? April went around the table and recovered the brochure from the floor. She looked down both directions of the aisle at clusters of families inspecting various displays of housewares.

It was time to become proactive.

With a deep inhale, she bellowed down the aisle, "Who's bored with their lives?"

Startled shoppers looked up, clearly not knowing how to respond. Some looked away; some at the aisle's end retreated around the corner. But a few paused and watched her. April gave the nervous audience her best smile and pointed toward her table.

"Leave the bathroom and kitchen remodel for next year. It's time for a holiday. One you've never experienced before."

One of the closer vendors glowered when a man pulled his companion away from a kitchen fixtures booth.

"C'mon," he said, dragging the shorter woman accompanying him toward April's table. "I'm tired of looking at sinks."

The couple reached the Ka Catchers' table, and April raised the volume on the slideshow. By then, a few other shoppers began to take tentative steps closer. The woman pulled free of her partner's grip and picked up a brochure.

"What kind of vacations are you selling?"

"Time travel."

"You're joking." She dropped the brochure and gave Mr. Tired-of-Sinks a smirk that said, *Can we please go now?*

But he seemed unperturbed. "Virtual reality theme park, right? Like Six Flags or Disney World."

April picked up the discarded brochure and placed it in his hands. "Nope. *Real* time travel. "

The woman rolled her eyes and said, "But it's not possib –"

"Hey, we saw a commercial about this on TV last week," he said. "Catcher something. Figured it was some gimmicky promotion."

April gestured to the banner running across the table. "Ka Catchers." She turned to his partner. "You want to see baths, try ancient Pompeii."

"You've been there?" She still sounded unconvinced.

119

Nodding, April lied, "Swam in the Roman pools myself. The mosaics are spectacular."

That's when she noticed the finely braided gold chain around her male partner's neck and the expensive gold wristwatch o his arm. And she sported designer Nikes that must have set her back a couple hundred. Maybe April would score at this show after all. Anyone remodeling a bathroom probably owned a house, and that meant disposable income. Vacation income.

Mr. Gold Chain-and-Wristwatch said, "Wasn't Pompeii the place with all the brothels?"

That earned him an elbow in the ribs from his companion. "You wish. But it's also the place that volcano covered up."

April was already on script. "The great thing about history is that you already know what happened – and how to avoid those sorts of things. And talk about a destination getaway. Pompeii was the go-to hotspot for jetsetters even before there were jets."

Ms. Nikes picked up the brochure again. "Any specials for twosomes?"

"I think that can be arranged." *If you want to take the risk. Look what happened to me.* They hadn't known until the past week a second person would travel to the same place as the first. There was still so much they didn't understand about The Time Portal. Perhaps they had jumped into this business a bit too soon. So many unanswered questions about how the thing worked.

"Got a card?" the woman asked.

April handed her a Ka Catchers business card. "I'm authorized to give you a travel show discount if you sign up today."

Shaking her head, the woman said, "Uh-uh. Not today." She grabbed her partner's arm and pushed him back toward the sinks. "But we'll think about it."

Seemed to be the story of their whole enterprise. She peered down the aisle and realized a whole new herd of potential clients were window shopping in adjacent booths.

She took a deep breath and shouted at the latest throng, "Who's bored with kitchenware and bathtubs?"

MICAH squirted glass cleaner on the limo's brand new windshield and wiped a rag across the surface. By the end of the first week of operation, Ka Catchers saw only one other Day Trip, and that was the comp promised to the county commissioner. Micah and April had sweated bullets all that day because of what had happened to Mr. Smith.

They sweated even bigger bullets when the State Department had called the day after Mr. Smith's scheduled appointment, looking for him. Micah didn't hear the other side of the phone call, only Buford's.

"Naw, he didn't show for his appointment," Buford had told them. "Can't say... Nope... Can't help you."

Lucky for Ka Catchers, the commissioner's Day Trip went well. April had steered the man to a safe place and period in history. For some reason, she'd suggested he travel to ancient Pompeii. He returned as scheduled, smiling like a fool and mumbling about hot baths and even hotter babes.

Now, besides the Smith/Cracker Jack fiasco, they had to worry about making money. April figured they'd set the price too high and should lower the cost of Day Trips. Buford refused. If people would pay six grand for a boring cruise, why wouldn't they pay a little more for the trip of a lifetime? At least, that was Buford's argument. He'd sure changed his tune from when they'd first started organizing Ka Catchers.

But Buford still had to pay for the Ectomobile. While they waited for bookings, he decided to open the ghost tours to anyone off the street.

Perry walked out of the Welcome Center and sauntered over to the limo. "Got her all cleaned up?"

"As shiny as mucous. How many clients tonight?"

Perry shrugged. "Only five. Picking 'em up at the parking lot outside Alien Landing. Want to ride along?"

Micah had never visited the local "haunts," and it was April's turn to watch Cracker Jack. He started to slide into the front passenger side when a dark green Lexus pulled into the drive. Lela stepped out of the car carrying a brown sack.

She called to her husband, "You forgot your snacks."

Perry met her in front of the Ectomobile and pecked his wife on the cheek. "Thanks, Pumpkin. All that ghost hunting might rev up my appetite."

About that time, the Welcome Center door flew open, and Buford lumbered out waving the chauffeur's cap.

"Don't leave without this!" He stopped in his tracks when he saw Lela. "What's she doing here?"

"*She* is bringing Perry something to eat since you're too cheap to buy him dinner," she shouted. "And quit talking like I'm not here."

Buford tossed the cap in Perry's direction and fled back into the Welcome Center.

Perry walked Lela to the Lexus, and Micah overheard him say, "Wouldn't hurt to cut the guy a little slack. Remember, I'm getting a free Day Trip out of this."

Micah couldn't hear Lela's response as she got back in the car, but he bet it wasn't complimentary. He'd taken an instant liking to her when she showed up at Ka Catcher's open house. The way she handled Buford was nothing short of amazing.

Perry crawled behind the steering wheel and stuffed the chauffeur's cap under the seat, winking at Micah.

Micah said, "*Your* wife doesn't seem to think much of *our* boss."

"Nope. They go back a long way and, believe me, there's no love lost between them. Mix about as well as oil and water." He started the Chrysler and pulled out of the driveway. "She thinks giving ghost tours is gonna be a bust. Lela gets most things right, but I think it'll be a hoot."

Where did Perry come up with all these corny expressions? Micah knew the only reason the Ectomobile's new chauffeur had agreed to give the tours was for the free time travel. He twisted in the seat to face the driver. "Decided when you're going on your Day Trip?"

"Well, since business is pretty slow, thought I might go soon."

"Where to?"

Perry turned onto the highway leading to Silverville. He seemed to think about the question. "Not sure where yet, but thinking of going into the future."

The Ka Catcher team had already talked about this. Sooner or later someone was going to try it, but they'd all planned to discourage the idea. Too many unknown variables. "I wouldn't."

Perry grinned. "There's got to be a pioneer for every new venture. Besides, I've been to a lot of places, done a lot of crazy things. Time to go where no one has gone before."

"No telling what you might find. We don't even know if it's possible – or how The Time Portal would react. I'm really uncomfortable with that, and Buford will freak out. Consider an alternative. Please."

Already pulling into Alien Landing, Perry said, "Okay, I'll think on it." They rolled to a stop as five tourists walked toward the Ectomobile. "There's our group."

A thirtysomething couple stood on either side of a youngster eating cotton candy. Two smart-ass punks about fifteen or sixteen a few steps behind pointed at the limo and laughed. The guy had a t-shirt that read "I'm from Zoo York" and a mini-Mohawk that looked stupid. The girl with him wore so much make-up Micah wondered if she was planning to hunt for tricks instead of ghosts.

Perry got out and withdrew a script from his pocket. Glancing at the words, he said, "Welcome to Ka Catchers' Ghost Tours, the most terrifying experience on the Western Slope." He paused and looked at the paper again. "Anyone with a heart condition must sign a waiver before we can begin."

No one raised a hand or came forward.

Perry held the script to his face and frowned as he looked closer at the wording. He stuffed it back in his pocket. "Aw, hell, let's just go."

Micah opened the door to the rear passenger compartment and their guests climbed in. Perry eased out of the parking lot, driving toward downtown. All the "haunted" locations on the tour lay within a six-block radius, making the need for a limo ridiculous, but Buford had demanded they use their pricey ride between each stop.

They wheeled up to the building that held the Elks Lodge. Piling out of the vehicle, the troupe clustered outside the front door.

Perry yanked out his script and read, "We ask everyone to be respectful as we enter the solemn inner sanctum for this noble organization. No matter what happens, please refrain from screaming."

The teenagers snorted, but the couple with the child gave each other nervous looks. Perry escorted them inside, where a short man in a blue blazer and gold sash greeted them.

"Welcome to the Benevolent and Protective Order of Elks, or B.P.O.E for short." He folded his hands in front of his chest, which reminded Micah of an undertaker. "Please walk this way."

The punks giggled and also folded their hands. The entire group followed him past a fancy wooden bar with a row of liquor bottles stacked against the wall behind. They climbed a dark stairwell that opened into a large high-ceilinged meeting room covering much of the building's second floor.

Even with the poor lighting, Micah could make out the silhouettes of elk heads mounted around the walls. *Creepy.* At the far end of the room stood three high-backed chairs and a podium on a small stage. Along the perimeter – sandwiched between the elk heads – gold plaques displayed name after name. Smaller chairs lined the walls, leaving most of the hall as empty as a roller skating rink. A single table draped in purple cloth sat in the center.

Their host's voice echoed in the space. "The Elks began in 1868. The club adopted the symbol of the elk because it is a creature of stature, and indigenous to America. The original members voted in favor of the elk instead of the buffalo." He walked below a huge head with antlers and pointed up.

The animal's glass eyes seemed to stare accusingly at Micah, and he turned away.

The Elks officer continued, "Although early members were mostly theatrical performers in New York City, the organization has since grown into a significant American fraternal and charitable service order with more than a million members."

"But where's the ghost?" one of the teen punks asked.

Looking puzzled, their guide scratched his chin. "Ghost?"

"Yeah, isn't this place haunted?"

"Well... I think somebody did mention they saw a ghost here, but that was years ago. Now, if I could direct your attention to the names of Exalted Rulers featured on the plaques surrounding you."

Micah nudged Perry, whispering, "I think this part of our ghost tour is done."

Perry must have thought so, too. "Thank You," he interrupted. "We have to move on to our next stop."

As they descended the stairs, Micah resisted the urge of tripping the smart-ass kids on the way down. Maybe bad for business.

Once they'd ushered everyone back into the limo, Mohawk Boy groaned, "That was really lame."

Perry drove them around two blocks before parking in front of the Silverville Arts Center, across the street from the Elks Lodge. Inside, a chunky, middle-aged woman showed them around the facilities but, in Micah's opinion, the only interesting feature was the tunnel in the basement – now caved in – that once secretly led to an 1800s brothel next door.

No ghosts, though.

The next stop at a bed & breakfast uncovered no paranormal entities either, but at least a few good stories and a cold spot in a hallway. They barely made it out before one of their guests knocked over and broke an antique lamp. The B&B owner seemed anxious to get them out the door, and Micah expected a call the next day asking Buford to cover damages.

The final destination of the evening was the old livery, now turned into a t-shirt shop. Legend told that one of Silverville's early sheriffs had died on the premises.

When they arrived, the door was locked and the building dark.

Micah asked Perry, "Isn't the owner supposed to meet us here?"

"That was the plan but, then again, we're ahead of schedule. You have the number to call?"

Buford had given them the phone numbers for all the stops since the tour was taking place after normal business hours. When Micah called, the voice on the other end answered with a sleepy "Hello."

"Is this L.T. Liverless?"

"Yeah." Silence.

"This is Ka Catchers. We scheduled a tour at your shop tonight."

Another long pause. "Oh yeah." A yawn. "I need to air up my bicycle tire first, and then I'll be right down. Be about 20 minutes."

Micah pressed the end-call button and gave Perry the bad news.

"Well, folks," Perry said to the group, "you're going to have a few minutes to stretch your legs and wander through downtown while we wait."

"But the shops are all closed," the thirtysomething woman said.

Perry nodded his head toward the bar next door. "Well, they're not all closed. You could go in there for your favorite beverage."

The teen punks headed in that direction, but Perry grabbed Mohawk Boy's collar and pulled him back. "Not you two."

"Hey," the kid barked. "Get your hands off me, or my old man will sue."

Perry kept his cool and let go.

Mohawk turned to Micah. "What do you do around here for fun?"

Micah thought for a minute. It seemed like an idiotic question. There were plenty of things to do in Silverville. "We've got a pretty good library. There's the observatory at night, of course. And during the day, you can rent canoes, go horseback riding or hiking ."

Make-Up Girl looked blank. "You mean like *walking*?"

"Yeah, Bimbo," said Mohawk Boy. "Like what you do at the mall."

"Where is your mall?" she asked.

Two hundred fifty miles away. "We don't have one."

Her jaw dropped. She turned to Mohawk Boy and mouthed, "No mall?"

The little boy with the couple whined that he had to pee, and Perry told him to go behind the limo. When the mother scowled at this suggestion, he told her it was either that or take the kid into the bar.

While they waited for the tinkling sound to stop, Micah noticed a strong, sweet smell wafting from the direction of the chainsaw sculpture of a bear in front of the t-shirt shop. On the animal's shoulders perched Mohawk Boy, sucking on a joint.

"Down from there!" Perry marched to the base of the sculpture. "And put out that, uh, smoke."

"It's legal in Colorado."

"But not on my ghost tours. Put that out, or I'll tell your dad."

The boy let out a long stream of smoke and croaked, "That's who I got it from."

While the argument continued, Micah heard the child behind him shriek.

Then the punk on the bear shouted, "Hey, man. Did you see that?" He dropped his joint and clung to the sculpture with one hand and pointed to the t-shirt shop with the other. "There's someone in there, staring at us through the window."

"And it's a cowboy!" shouted the little kid.

Everyone turned to look, but the window was empty.

Mohawk Boy dropped to the sidewalk. "I swear it! There was someone in there looking out at us!"

At that moment, a recurring squeaking sound grew louder from down the street.

L.T. Liverless rode up on an ancient townie bike – the same color as the Ektomobile – dropped his kickstand, and sauntered over to the group with a slightly bow-legged shuffle. "Sorry 'bout that. I fell asleep."

He combed sandy-colored hair with his fingers and scuffed mud off his cowboy boots. Unlocking the door, he flipped on the lights and went inside. Everyone crowded in behind him.

"I'm not sure this will be what you expected," he said.

"Does-does anybody live here at night?" stuttered the stoner punk.

Liverless shrugged. "Sometimes one of my workers stays late. But not tonight. Why?"

Perry said, "Two of our guests thought they saw someone through the glass."

"Probably a reflection. Street lights, passing car."

"No," Stoner Boy said, "I saw someone – or something."

"A ghost with a cowboy hat," the little boy added.

"Uh-huh." Liverless sounded unimpressed.

The little boy's father said, "But your shop is on the tour."

"Yeah, well, I guess there are stories about Mr. Jangles. You know, the sound of spurs on the second floor? But I've had this shop for years, and I've never, ever heard or seen anything."

Liverless spread his arms and turned around in a full circle.

Perry said, "Why don't you tell them the story about Mr. Jangles."

"Not much to tell. All I know is a sheriff was supposedly murdered in this building in the 1800s. A few folks say they've seen or heard him. Not me."

Perry kept pushing. "Isn't there a red stain on the floor?"

"Oh that. Yeah."

"Can we see it?" the child's father asked.

"No. I put a display case over it."

Everyone groaned.

"Well, that's about it. Got any more questions?"

The little boy jumped up and down. "I want to see the ghost again!"

"Look, kid," Liverless said. "There's no such thing as ghosts. And there's no Santa Claus either."

The mother gasped and covered her child's ears. But it was too late. The kid had heard it and started to cry.

Well, thought Micah, *at least the ghost tour wasn't a total bust.*

DID A field trip count as a date?

April couldn't decide. Maybe – at least for someone like Micah. Either way, she found herself hiking with him toward an old mine.

"April," he'd asked the previous day, "wanna do something – I mean, go outside, or..."

At first, she figured he needed help outside the Welcome Center. "Can't right now. I'm trying to straighten out Ka Catchers' bills."

"Um, that's not what I meant," he'd stammered.

She looked up from the paperwork. "What then?"

"Would you like to go on a ... field trip ... with me? I know you like history and there's some cool old silver mines around here."

The very fact he'd built up the nerve to ask surprised her. Okay, it wasn't exactly romantic, but *he'd* asked first. A start, anyway.

Two days later, she found herself pushing through sagebrush and into a clearing of tall grass, tugging at the pig's leash and trying to keep up with Micah's long legs. Poor Breakfast complained constantly. They'd thought she might enjoy the outing. She didn't.

"Slow down!" April called ahead. "Breakfast needs a break."

"We're here." Micah stopped next to a padlocked gate that held a no-trespassing sign. "The mine's over the next hill."

A three-strand barbed wire fence stretched on either side of the gate, continuing in opposite directions as far as the eye could see. Walking to the wire sagging between two nearby fence posts, he pried apart two strands and helped her and the pig scramble through. When they cleared the fence, he followed.

"Are we gonna get in trouble?" April asked.

"Naw, I doubt anybody's been here for fifty years."

They tracked along the two parallel paths running through the gate that must have led to the mine. Along the old road ruts, the sage played out and turned into sparse grass, making it easier for the pig to trot along. When they topped the hill, April looked down into a bowl that held several ramshackle buildings and sheds arranged in no particular order. Looked like the miners threw up the shacks anywhere the ground was flat enough. A single wooden structure towered above everything else.

Pointing, April asked, "What's that tall thing?"

"A derrick. It's over the main mine shaft. You'll see what I mean in a few minutes."

As they picked their way down the slope, April noticed small patches of wildflowers and blooming cactus snugged against the boulders on either side of the trail. She could smell a spicey, woody fragrance every time her pant leg brushed against the sage growing alongside the path. Above the bowl's rim, the sky shone a deep blue except for a few cottony clouds.

She stopped and took in the scenery.

"What're you doing?"

She smiled. "Just seems like a perfect day."

Micah backtracked to stand beside her. "Yeah, it does."

When she caught him staring at her instead of the scenery, his face turned red.

To keep the moment from turning awkward, she blurted out, "You hungry yet? We've been hiking a couple of hours." She let

131

her backpack slide off her shoulder and rummaged inside. "You want a peanut butter sandwich, raisins, or granola mix?"

They settled on a flat rock and divided up the food. She tossed Breakfast a carrot.

Munching on the snacks, April asked, "Who built all this? And when did it close?"

He swallowed. "Uh, miners, I guess. It's been shut down for a long time."

"So this is a silver mine?"

"I think so. But they mined uranium around here, too."

She thought about this as she tossed the pig another carrot. Evidently, he knew less about the area than she did. She'd have to go by the library and dig through some old maps. "Isn't uranium poisonous?"

"Must be. Last time I was here, I found a shack covering a pond with blind white fish swimming around. But that could've happened from the uranium in the soil."

She stood. "C'mon. I want to see those fish."

They covered the final two hundred yards to the old operation. The closer they got, the more they saw trash scattered among the vegetation. Old rusty cans, a few shattered jars, unidentifiable metal scraps, and broken tools.

April picked up a small glass bottle lodged in the dirt and brushed it off. To her surprise, the little container was still intact and had a tiny round wooden cap.

"What's that?" Micah asked, stepping closer.

"Not sure." The shape looked like a little glass angel with a pleated robe but no wings. She turned it over and squinted at the engraving on the bottom. *Helena Rubinstein, 1941, New York Distributor.* "Looks like a perfume bottle." She waggled the little container. "Why would miners have this?"

He shrugged. "Present for a girlfriend?"

"It's mine now." April clutched the perfume bottle and walked toward the nearest building. Inside, they found shelves holding rows of foot-long rock cylinders. Core samples, Micah told her. She squatted, setting her bottle down, and reached into a cubbyhole to pull one out. "Wow, these are heavy."

At that moment, Breakfast snatched the bottle from the floor and started to run.

"Hey! That's no carrot. Micah, grab that pig!"

The squeal reverberated off the walls of the old shack as he grabbed a hind foot disappearing out the door. "Gotcha!" He reeled the pig back inside, pried the bottle out of her mouth, and handed it to April.

She shook a finger at Breakfast. "Bad pig, bad."

The animal's corkscrew tail wagged back and forth. She didn't look contrite.

"Lemme show you those fish."

Micah led her across the mining grounds to a larger rectangular building. The door stood ajar, and she started inside.

He blocked her with his arm. "Hold it. The pool fills most the space, and there's a walkway along one wall. But it's narrow and there's no railing. So be careful."

She nodded and snugged the pig's leash closer, edging through the entrance. Dirty windows partially illuminated the creepy interior, just enough to see the dilapidated planks of a boardwalk three feet above murky water.

"I don't see anything."

"Squat down and wait," he said from the door.

She did, peering into the dark pool. "Aren't you coming?" she called over her shoulder.

"Once was enough for me. I don't like water when I can't see the bottom."

After a minute or two, her eyes began to adjust to the dingy light, and she thought she saw a pale shape the length of her forearm whisk by. "Oh! I saw something." Another ghostly fish swam past, even closer to the surface. "My God, they don't have eyes!"

She set the perfume bottle down next to her and braced both hands on the planking to lean further over the edge – when a blur of pig ducked behind her. Breakfast dived at the bottle, but April plucked it from the plank before the pig could reach it. Focused on her prize, Breakfast overshot her target and slid into the pool.

In horror, April screamed for Micah, watching the pig flounder and struggle. *Could pigs even swim?* She had no idea. *Did mutant fish eat pork?*

Micah was beside her in an instant, reaching down to find a hold on Breakfast. But the pig's skin was too tight, nothing to grasp. She kept slipping out of his hands.

"That's not working," April shouted. "I'm going in to help her."

"No you're not." He yanked off his boots and jumped in.

April gasped when his head disappeared under the water.

Then he stood up and started to laugh. "It's only four feet deep."

Breakfast paddled over to him. *Guess pigs can swim after all.*

He tugged her next to the boardwalk and tried to hoist her up to April, but it didn't work. No way Micah could scoop up a hundred pounds of wet pig and deadlift her into April's arms. She leaned further over to get a better grip and heaved to lift Breakfast.

This might just work.

Instead, she felt the walkway giving way underneath her, and she released the pig just in time to roll onto firmer planks. Micah and the pig splashed back into the water.

"You guys okay?"

"Yeah," he said, looking at the collapsed boardwalk. "This might be even better."

The broken boards had sagged so much they created a ramp into the pool. Micah pushed and April tugged until they maneuvered the pig out of the water. She took Breakfast outside and tied her leash to a post before returning to help Micah.

"Okay, your turn." She leaned down and extended a hand while he slipped and scrambled up the wet boards. At the last moment of his rescue, his feet went out from under him and he lunged for her support, sending her backwards and Micah on top.

They stared at each other, their faces a mere two inches apart. April didn't know whether to laugh or kiss him. She opted for the latter.

It lasted until Breakfast started squealing a protest outside.

APRIL looked out the window. "There's more of them coming."

Buford groaned. "Have they set foot on my property yet?"

She shook her head no.

Since nine o'clock that morning, Brother Martin's fanatical little religious group had grown in numbers by the hour. Looked like they had erected an open-sided canvas awning within feet of Ka Catchers' driveway. Someone was pulling sound equipment out of a minivan and setting it up next to a generator under the tent. Already, an old lady had started to strike a tambourine, chanting in rhythm to her thumps, "Thou shalt not transgress! Thou shalt not transgress!"

Damn them all. April had planned to sleep in that Sunday morning after a tough sales day at another trade show. But Buford's frantic call pulled her out of bed to help him drive the lunatic evangelists from the gates.

The commotion drove Breakfast crazy, and she ran in tight circles, rooting against the door and snorting.

Micah burst into the Welcome Center reception room. "Gotta be twenty-five more cars coming this direction down the highway."

"What do these crazy fools want?" Buford asked.

April peered out the window in time to see two men unfurl a large banner that read, "BUFORD PRICE WILL BURN."

She pointed outside. "Apparently, they intend to send you to hell."

Halfway down the drive, Howard and Cracker Jack Smith stood gaping at the makeshift revival. Howard clapped his hands in time with the tambourine.

Buford cracked the door open wide enough to shout, "Get in here, you idiots!"

Micah had been right. The approaching cars pulled off the road next to the driveway, and a crowd soon swelled around a tall, thin man in a black frock coat. April figured this must be Brother Martin. He led his flock under the awning, stepped up to a podium, and raised a bullhorn to his lips. "Brothers, sisters, we have important work to do here today. The Lord's work."

Volleys of "Amens!" erupted as Martin gathered momentum. "The Book of Ecclesiastes records, 'There is a time for everything, and a season for every activity under the heavens: a time to be born and a time to die, a time to plant and a time to uproot, a time to kill and a time to heal.'"

His other hand brandished what had to be Bible. "And now it's time to tear down that infernal time machine!"

Buford eyes widened. "No, I think it's time to call the sheriff." He backed away from the window, falling butt-first over the pig. "April, get on the phone and tell Carl to get over here."

She dialed 9-1-1.

After two rings, a dispatch operator answered, "State your emergency."

There's a man on the floor wrestling a pig. We have a brain-dead zombie who won't eat anything but donuts and caramel corn. And there's a minister preaching hellfire and damnation at the door. "We have a crowd of protesters out at Ka Catchers, and it looks like they might get violent. Can you send the sheriff over right away?"

She heard the dispatcher clunk the phone on the desk and whisper in the background. A moment later, the voice returned. "Uh, the sheriff's not here right now. He's fishing."

"Well, can you send somebody else then?"

More whispers.

"Ma'am, I'm not sure who's close enough to respond. I can make a few phone calls."

April snapped the cell phone shut. "The sheriff's not available, but they'll see if they can find somebody else to come out."

Buford scrambled to his feet. "What the hell! What am I paying taxes for?"

He barely finished his complaining when a dark Crown Vic pulled into the driveway, scattering the faithful, and drove up to the Welcome Center.

Buford said, "Boy, that was quick."

Three men emerged from the vehicle and made their way to the door. None wore police uniforms but instead dark suits and ties. They didn't look like anybody from Silverville, but one of them seemed familiar.

They knocked on the front door and waited rather than coming inside. Odd behavior, and a bit formal for these parts.

"Answer the door," Buford said.

April stepped to the entrance and let them in.

Buford rushed over to the two men who came in first. "Thank God you're here! You've got to do something about those people before they tear down The Time Portal."

"Uh, Buford," April said, "I don't think they're here for crowd control."

"Huh?" Then his eyes fell on the third and biggest man. Bentu. The goon who'd accompanied Mr. Smith when he'd made his appointment for the Day Trip.

In a panic, April spun around to find Howard and Cracker Jack, but Micah must have already assessed the situation and ushered them out the back.

Buford pointed at Bentu. "What's he doing here?"

One of the other men flashed a badge. "I'm Agent Latimer with the State Department." He gestured to the man next to him, who also showed a badge. "This is my colleague, Agent Pearl. We've asked Mr. Bentu to accompany us in our investigation."

Oh shit.

"I don't understand," Buford said, looking from one to the other.

"Are you Buford Price, owner of Ka Catchers?" Agent Latimer asked. The other agent pulled out a tape recorder and switched it on.

"Well, yes. What's this all about?"

Through the window at the agents' backs, Micah was helping Cracker Jack onto a bicycle and motioned for him to follow Howard, who started pedaling away.

Latimer pulled a photograph from his coat. "Have you seen this man?"

"Mr. Smith?" Buford asked.

The agents exchanged amused glances. Latimer continued, "That may be what he called himself, but his real name is Abdul-Qadir, prince of the House of Al Shamie." The agent let that sink in. "Mr. Price, this is a missing person's investigation. He was last seen early on Tuesday morning, five days ago. We understand he had an appointment here on Thursday."

138

"He did – I mean, he didn't – I mean, he never showed up." Buford grabbed April by the shoulders and shoved her in between him and agents like a human shield. "Tell them, April. Tell them how he never showed up."

She wriggled free of his grasp and swallowed hard. "He's right. Mr. Smith, er, Prince Abdul did have an appointment on Thursday, but he didn't make it."

"We also know he wrote a check to your company for the amount of $10,000. Can you confirm that?"

At this, Buford broke in. "We don't give any refunds, if that's what you're getting at."

April turned to face Buford and mouthed, *Shut up*. Then she faced the agents again. "Yes, he did write a check in advance, during our open house."

The men studied the room and its occupants. Latimer asked, "Does anyone else work here?"

"Just me," Micah said, coming into the room from the back.

Latimer showed him the photo and asked him if he had seen the man.

To his credit, Micah never skipped a beat. "Yes, sir, the day of the open house. But not since then."

Latimer said nothing for several seconds, staring at the Ka Catcher team through narrowed eyes. "I'll need statements from each of you, with detailed accounts of your whereabouts since last Tuesday."

"Are we under some sort of suspicion?" Buford asked nervously.

"No, Mr. Price. This is routine procedure – particularly for such a high-profile case."

"High profile? I've never heard of this guy before," Buford said.

Latimer nodded. "Good."

Agent Pearl took them one by one into an adjoining room to take their statements. When April's turn came, for once she told the truth about everywhere she'd been – with the exception of going to ancient Turkey shortly after Mr. Smith's Day Trip began. And that was only a half lie since her body stayed in the outhouse.

The statements complete, April saw Micah duck outside as the agents began to pack up.

Latimer said, "Before we leave, we'd like to have a look around."

They didn't wait for permission but walked out the door and started toward The Time Portal.

Latimer & Company only made it several yards before a large delegation of Holy Grail followers intercepted them halfway to the outhouse's outer gate.

"Hey!" Buford said. "Those Bible-thumpers are trespassing."

Micah snickered. "It's okay. I told them our guests were interested in joining the church."

Brother Martin and his group swarmed around the State Department officials like shoppers to a Walmart blue-light special. The agents held up their badges. April couldn't hear the conversation, but the Feds looked uncomfortable and began edging their way back to the car.

"No worries, Buford," April said. "They can't make it to the outhouse now. They're leaving."

She sighed with relief. Did they suspect anything? She didn't think so, but she hoped Howard and Cracker Jack wouldn't show back up until after the agents left.

Lucky for Ka Catchers, they didn't. In fact, Cracker Jack hadn't come back at all.

CHAPTER SEVEN

"So, where's Cracker Jack?" Micah asked Howard.

"He's still eating his ice cream."

"What do you mean? Where's he at?"

While he spoke with Howard, Micah noticed Buford walking from window to window. The chanting from the crowd outside had grown louder.

Howard cupped his hands around his mouth. "What? Can't hear you."

"Cracker Jack, where *is* he?"

"Oh, Alien Landing. We stopped there for snacks."

"And you just left him there?" April asked. "He'll never find his way back."

The din made by the protesters dropped to a momentary lull.

Buford stopped pacing long enough to say, "Atta boy, Howard. That's one less freeloader to worry about."

Micah looked at Buford in horror. He had no idea how helpless Cracker Jack was. "You can't be serious."

Howard grinned. "Don't worry. I gave him directions."

Buford waved his hand to dismiss the whole conversation. "I got bigger things to worry about. I'm going out there to talk to Brother Martin."

"Think it's safe?" asked April.

"You're right." Buford yanked Howard by the arm and pushed him out the door first.

Once they left the Center, Micah went to the desk where they kept the Ectomobile keys. "I better go find him."

"Let's talk about this for a minute," April said.

"Talk about it?" He looked at Breakfast, who lay snoring in the corner. "He's not even as smart as that pig."

"We might be better off if he doesn't come back."

"But we're responsible for him."

"Yeah, and we can go to jail because of him, too. If he can't find his way home, no one can pin it on us."

Micah couldn't believe his ears. "It's even worse because you *know* who he is, and you know why he's a zombie. You sound just like Buford."

April gasped, her face losing color. For a few moments, she said nothing. "Oh, God, Micah, you're right. I can't believe I said that. You know I'm not like him. I just thought, with the Feds coming here –"

Movement outside caught both their attention. Pressing her face against the window, April said, "Look, the crowd's breaking up. And Brother Martin is shaking Buford's hand!"

Micah joined her at the window in time to see Buford and Howard walking back to the Welcome Center. Behind them, the congregation began packing up the sound equipment and striking the tent awning.

When Buford stepped inside, April asked, "How'd you pull that off?"

Buford puffed up his chest. "Capitalist ingenuity. Listen and learn. I offered Martin a cut on any Day Trip taken to the Holy Land. Fifty percent."

April looked puzzled. "Can we afford that?"

"Sure can – if you scare people out of ever visiting there. Tell them they'll get leprosy or something." His eyes moved toward the keys in Micah's hands. "Where you going with my limo?"

Micah opened his mouth to make some excuse when April jumped in. "Gonna take it to the car wash before the next ghost tour." She took the keys out of Micah's hands. "My turn to drive."

As they walked out the door, she leaned toward Micah and whispered, "And we'll pick up a passenger at Alien Landing along the way."

AT FIRST, April thought she looked cool. The lacy, low-cut gown showed just enough cleavage to be sexy. Below the waist, the gathered bunting and bows were downright decadent. But after an hour walking downtown Silverville as Marie Antoinette, she'd changed her mind. The corset and powdered wig were way too hot for July. And the pummel that ballooned the dress at the hips took up so much room that Micah couldn't even walk beside her. Oncoming tourists had to press themselves against buildings – or else step into the gutter – to let her pass.

She drew lots of attention, but then that was the whole idea.

"Criminy, my feet hurt." She lifted her skirt and looked at her pointy, tight slippers.

"At least you don't have to parade around in leotards," Micah said, blowing at the limp feather that drooped from the top of his green cap.

His outfit included a belted leather tunic that barely covered his butt, green tights, and high boots with turned-down cuffs. A buckled sash ran diagonally across his chest, supporting a quiver full of arrows at his back.

143

April was pretty sure the real Robin Hood didn't dress like Errol Flynn, but that's what the costume company sent. Actually, it made him look kind of sexy.

To all passersby, Micah pressed a flyer promoting Ka Catchers and the ghost tours into their hands. A few expressed genuine interest in hunting for spirits. But most seemed skeptical about The Time Portal. Some even laughed.

"Is this a joke?" one guy asked, leading a schnauzer. He looked as ridiculous as Micah. But in his case, a tinfoil hat and Alien Landing t-shirt. "I'm here for the alien stuff, not fake time travel."

April batted her eyes and fluttered her fan. Taking on the persona of her costume's namesake, she replied in a passable French accent, "Indeed, sir, it is not. *C'est vrai.*"

"Huh?"

She lowered her fan and dropped her accent. "It's real. Haven't you seen the commercials?"

"Sure, but I figured it was some sort of virtual reality game."

"Nope, as real as your little gray dog." April nudged the pooch away from her dress with a slipper.

"Well how much is it?"

"A bargain, considering what you'll see."

Micah interrupted, "Ten grand for twenty-four hours."

The tourist snorted. "Got to be kidding. C'mon, Dusty.... Dusty?"

The leash led under April's skirt. When she tried to step back, the movement jerked the leash from the man's hand, followed by a sharp yelp.

"You stealing my dog?" He stooped and started to raise her skirt.

Robin Hood leaped to her rescue. "Hey, buddy, no peeking under the lady's dress." Micah grabbed the man by the back of the collar and pulled him to the side.

Her escort was sort of cute when he tried to be chivalrous. The more time she spent with Micah, the more she decided he might have hidden potential – if she could just get him to loosen up a bit.

Dusty began to whine as Micah turned his head away and reached beneath the bunting and bows. "His head's stuck in the, uh, cage holding up your dress. Wait, I think I can get him out."

By now, a small group of people clustered around the scene. April took the opportunity to pass out flyers while Micah struggled to free the schnauzer.

Within a minute, Micah tumbled backwards, the dog landing on his chest. Onlookers cheered.

"My hero!" April crooned and curtsied. Then she pulled Micah to his feet and whispered, "Let's get the hell outta here."

People clapped at what they probably thought was a staged street performance. As Micah and April started to walk away, a small group of teenaged girls clustered around Robin Hood, making a fuss over his costume. The one in butt-exposing tight shorts kept touching his sash, cap, quiver. In fact, her hands were all over him.

She said, "Wow, you sure have a big arrow. Can I hold it?"

To April, it seemed like he enjoyed the attention a bit too much. She wedged in between him and the little harlot and thrust extra flyers into his hands. "Hey, you should take some of these into the T-shirt shop."

"Oh, sure, I can do that." He bent in a mock bow before he walked toward the store.

When the girl started to follow, April cut her off and moved close to her ear.

"Back off," she hissed. "He's taken."

The girl looked stunned. "What?"

"You know what I'm talking about. Beat it."

The gaggle of girls had disappeared when Micah returned. "Where is ... everybody?"

"Tracking their next victim."

Micah seemed clueless, of course. Men always were.

A block further down Main Street, they came upon the Lazy S Diner. Micah held the door open while April side-stepped and squeezed through the entrance. They took one look at the narrow benches in the booths and simultaneously moved toward the bar stools.

"Micah, help me," April said, trying to lift her dress over a seat.

He lifted one side of the pummel over the stool to her left and then did the same to the stool on her right. "Um, we're not close enough to talk." He glanced at a tall empty table with armless chairs situated in front of the window. "Let's move over there."

He helped her climb back off the stool, and they resettled at the window table. April let her pummel drop to either side of the chair. At the same time, she heard the dress's cage crack. Good. Having her head chopped off couldn't be worse than wearing this thing.

A waitress with a wandering eye approached with menus.

"We're just having lemonades, Fawn." Micah returned the menus, and the woman walked away.

"Wow, there're a lot of people in Silverville right now," April observed.

"Should have been here last summer. A film company shot a movie, *Silverville vs. the Flying Saucers.*"

"I don't remember that one."

He shrugged. "Never came out. At least, not yet. But sure caused a lot of buzz."

Fawn came with the lemonades.

Micah continued, "A few years ago, a couple of UFOs flew over town during the Fourth of July. You remember that, don't you, Fawn?"

Both Micah and April looked at their waitress. She stared back, an eye on each of them. After a moment, she nodded, set the drinks down, and walked off.

"Yeah, I'd heard that," April said. She stirred the ice in her lemonade. "Thanks for coming to my aid on the street. That was sweet."

Could have been the glare from the window, but it looked to her that his face turned red, like it had on their trip to the mine. What a puppy dog. Nothing like she'd expected that first day when she chewed him out about Howard. In some ways, she and Micah were sort of alike – both were social pariahs, both spent too much time with their heads in books, and both had trouble making friends. She was pretty certain he'd never had a romantic relationship before. Something else they had in common.

"Ever had a real girlfriend, Micah?"

He grinned and looked embarrassed, swiveling the lemonade glass on the coaster.

She didn't think so. "Would you like to?"

"You mean … you?"

"Well duh, Robin Hood. Unless you'd prefer to chase your merry men through Sherwood Forest."

The grin widened across his face.

"I'll take that as a yes." Then she waited for him to ask her out for real – not just for a "field trip," but he didn't. Okay, she'd have to be the one to pick a time and place. "Movie? Tomorrow night? There's still a drive-in over in Placer City."

"Sure."

Geez, starting a relationship with Micah turned out to be more work than she'd thought. She felt sweat tickling her scalp under the heavy wig. "Hey, give me one of your arrows."

He reached over his shoulder, plucked one from the quiver, and handed it to her. *Nice. At least he follows orders without question.*

She plunged the arrow, point first, into the side of her wig and began to scratch. "Off the subject, but we've got something else to talk about right now. Cracker Jack."

"You mean the guy you were gonna leave at Alien Landing?" he teased.

She pulled the arrow from her wig and tapped him on the head with the fletchings. "Hey, I wasn't really going to do that." *Okay, yeah, I was thinking about it.* "And we did go find him and bring him back. But now what?"

"Been wondering about that a lot ever since the Feds showed up yesterday." He grasped the arrow and pushed it back into his quiver. "Guess he's more than just a rich guy."

Or a brainless prince. As big a surprise as the leopard pouncing on and killing him. April had thought about it, too. She and Micah had to come up with a plan, and quick, before it snowballed into an international incident. Or maybe it already had.

Micah continued, "I think it's time to tell Buford."

"Why? So he can take Cracker Jack to the nearest cliff and push him off?"

"Think he'd really do that?"

April shrugged. She didn't know what Buford's response would be. To protect himself first, for sure. But to go as far as killing Cracker Jack? Probably not. He might dump the prince on a deserted road like an unwanted pet. And if the noose got too tight, he'd likely not hesitate to hand her and Micah over to Bentu to save his own skin.

"Naw, as slimy as Buford is, I don't think he'd hurt Cracker Jack. But he'd find another way to make him –" she hooked her fingers into quote marks "– disappear. Telling Buford's not the solution."

"Then what *do* we do? We gotta come up with ..." Micah took a deep breath and fell onto the floor.

For a moment, April stared, waiting for him to get back up and finish his sentence. But he didn't, nor did he move.

Something was wrong. She struggled to free her broken pummel from the chair, but it caught fast.

"Oh, hell."

Reaching under her skirts, she clutched the waist of the pummel, snapped it in half, and kicked off the rest of the splintered lattice. She stooped beside Micah, his eyes closed and his face a sickly white. She lifted his head and patted his cheek. "What's wrong?"

No response.

She slapped him harder. "Micah, wake up!"

The nearest Lazy S patrons got out of their chairs and crowded around.

She heard the waitress ask behind her, "Problem?"

"He won't wake up!" April shrieked.

"I'll call an ambulance," Fawn said.

AFTER the ambulance drove away, it took April less than five minutes to run to her little 1993 Ford "Empo" (the T had fallen off) and drive to the hospital's visitor parking lot. But once inside, she couldn't find him.

She went to the reception desk, panting, and asked, "Where's Micah Musil? Where's the emergency room?"

The woman behind the counter pointed to a corridor, and April took off, dragging her torn ribbons and bows after her. When she found ER, she demanded to see Micah.

"Are you a member of the family?" the emergency room nurse asked, staring at her powdered wig.

"Well no, but I was with him when – "

"Then you'll have to wait out here 'til the doctor is finished." She showed April the adjacent waiting area, which held only a couple of other people.

She plopped down into a vinyl and chrome chair and looked at the table of uninteresting magazines. She flipped through the top one on the stack, not even seeing the pictures. *Oh, Micah, what's wrong with you?* "Please, please let him be okay," she whispered to no one in particular.

Dropping the magazine, she stood and paced from one end of the room to the other. She ripped off the trailing bunting and threw it in the trash. The wig soon followed. None of that seemed to matter right now.

She walked back to the ER desk. "Can you at least tell me if he's going to be okay?"

"The doctor's still with him. Do you know how to get a hold of his family?"

Holy shit. This is serious. "Far as I know, he just has a mother."

"What is his home phone?"

She blurted out the numbers. "When can I see him?"

"When the doctor's finished, he has some questions for you."

The woman returned to her computer screen. April felt like she'd been dismissed.

She went back into the waiting room. Should she call Buford, or should she wait until she knew something? How long had Micah been in there now anyway? She looked at the wall clock. Ten minutes since she'd arrived at the hospital.

"Don't expect any answers soon."

April looked at a ragged woman sitting by a shopping basket in the corner of the room. "Excuse me?"

April had scarcely noticed her.

"I said," the woman repeated, "don't expect answers soon. I brought Uncle Al in here two hours ago, and no one will talk to me."

Her heart sank. Two hours! She'd go nuts in that time. Even if she wasn't family, she was *like* family. At least she cared. She spent the next half hour alternating between tearing off bits of her costume and ignoring the doomsayer with the shopping basket.

At last, a man in a white coat filled the doorway and strode in her direction. "Miss?"

April jumped up and met him halfway.

He stepped back a foot. "Are you the one who called the ambulance?"

"I was with him when this happened."

"We can't get hold of anyone at the number you gave us, but we'll keep trying. In the meantime, would you mind answering a few questions?"

"What's wrong with him? Is he going to be okay?"

He shook his head. "Sorry, I can't divulge that information. Patient privacy. I can tell you we're still running tests. It would help us if we knew what happened before he lost consciousness."

She related the events of that morning.

"Have you known him long? Has he shown any ... unusual symptoms?"

April thought about it for a moment. She couldn't recall anything, except ... "He's been coughing a lot. Sometimes looks a little pale, but he spends lots of time in front of a computer."

The doctor made a couple of notes. "Coughed up any blood?"

She tried to remember. Sometimes he did cough into a tissue, but he'd always stuffed it into his pocket. She figured he was just being polite. "Not that I know of."

"Anything else?'

She gestured helplessly.

"Okay, thanks." He turned to go.

"When can I see him?"

He stopped. "When he regains consciousness, we'll move him into a room."

"Then you think he'll be all right?"

"Too soon to tell."

APRIL looked at her watch. Six o'clock. She couldn't wait any longer.

She told Buford, "I'm going to try calling," and dialed the hospital. When she got through to the station nurse, April asked, "Can you please tell me if Micah Musil can have visitors yet?"

The nurse on the other end of the line asked April to hold while she checked the chart. A minute later, April heard the connection transfer to a ring.

A groggy Micah answered, "Hello?"

"Sounds like you're awake."

"Just barely."

"Can you have visitors now?"

Micah coughed into the receiver. "Think so."

"We'll be right there." She hung up.

Buford was squatting over a tangle of wires and cords behind the new flatscreen TV he'd set up in the Welcome Center. "We? I'm too busy right now. He's in good hands. Not like there's anything we can do for him."

What an asshole. She'd been disappointed in his lack of concern over Micah's health when she came back to Ka Catchers and told him what had happened. He got more worked up over her torn costume than for the employee who had collapsed downtown.

"Buford, I'm not going to tell you what I really think of you right now." She took the cords from his hands and latched onto his ear, pulling him up upright. "You're going."

"But who'll take care of the pig?"

"Breakfast can come along. We'll leave her in the car."

"Okay, then we're taking yours," he grumbled.

It took only fifteen minutes to drive to town, park, and wander a few halls to find Micah's room. Someone had raised the head of the hospital bed so Micah could half sit up on his pillows. IVs threaded from his arm to a hanging bottle, and a little plastic tube stuck in his nose for oxygen.

Buford took one look and turned to April. "See, I told you. He's fine."

She walked over to the bed and placed her hand over Micah's. "How're you feeling?"

He smiled. "Still pretty weak. The docs are running tests."

"Christ on a cupcake! You really scared me."

"Sorry." He reached for his water, but couldn't quite get hold of the cup and straw.

April pulled the tray closer and held the straw to his lips. "Why didn't you tell me you were this sick?"

He stopped sipping. "Just thought I had the summer flu."

"Can I get you anything else?"

"For Pete's sake!" Buford slouched into the chair beside the bed. "Kid's got it made. I bet he even has hot and cold running nurse service. Hey!" He jumped up and went over to the wall-mounted television to peer behind it. "Oh, that's where that cord goes."

April sat on the edge of the bed and asked, "Micah, has anyone gotten hold of your mother yet?"

"Yeah, she's with Glenn in Las Vegas. She called right before you got here. I told her not to come back early. I'll be out of here soon."

"That true?"

Micah's eyes moved toward the door. "Let's ask the doctor."

The same physician she'd talked to that morning entered the room. He walked to the foot of the bed and lifted a chart.

153

April waited for him to read the notes. "Do you know anything yet?"

The doctor glanced at his patient.

Micah nodded. "It's okay. They're like family."

"Buford," April scolded, "the doctor's here. Pay attention."

The physician held a penlight to Micah's eyes. "Well, young man, it's clear you have a respiratory infection. We're just not sure what kind yet. We've sent samples to the lab, and it'll be a couple days before we get anything definitive."

"But it's something you can fix, right?" April asked.

"We've placed him on a heavy regimen of antibiotics until we know more." To Micah, he asked, "Have you been out of the country in the last year? Particularly the Middle East?"

He shook his head and looked at April.

That was right. His body never left Silverville. His mind, on the other hand, had ranged all over the place – and time.

"Why?" April asked.

"Just ruling out an unlikely source. There's one strain of coronavirus that produces symptoms somewhat like Micah's. Mostly across the Middle East."

Buford interrupted, "We haven't been around anybody from the Middle East – except for …" His eyes widened and he turned to April and Micah. "Nah, we just met this one guy from over there for five minutes."

Of course, Cracker Jack. Living under the same roof, breathing the same air. Did he give this to Micah? Mr. Smith never seemed sick.

She asked the doctor, "Can someone be a carrier and not know it?"

"Doubtful. The symptoms are pronounced. The Middle Eastern strain is largely an unknown infectious agent, similar to SARS, and has been deadly. But Micah's symptoms suggest several more likely agents. It might even be an invasive histoplasmosis."

Micah gasped. "Whoa! That's sound pretty serious."

The doctor laughed. "Not unless you have a compromised immune system, and you don't. This common strain is easily treated."

"Whew!" Micah relaxed back against his pillow. But then he broke into a fit of coughing.

April studied his pasty face against the pillow case. "What about the uncommon strain?"

"Lethal. But I wouldn't worry about that. It's a rare fungus that adheres to human excrement. Only documented four times, and that was during an archaeological excavation of Roman latrines."

April slumped against the wall. *What kind of Karma is this? Just got my first boyfriend, and now he might die.*

BUFORD crouched behind the flatscreen TV, still trying to figure out how to tune in the reception. At the same time, he did his best to tune out April, who hadn't let up about Micah since they'd visited him yesterday. He concentrated on the back of the box, holding an extra wire and wondering where to plug it in.

The problem felt like his life right now. If only he could find a way to plug the idea of time travel into the public's mind. Ka Catchers had seemed like such an easy sell. Either he priced it too high or people didn't take it seriously. Much as he hated the thought, he might have to comp a few more Day Trips – that, or offer some discounts to get the business rolling.

Howard and that worthless Cracker Jack came in the door and made a beeline for the pig. Howard had taken a real shine to the animal, trying to teach it tricks. Or at least he thought so. The one that got Buford was when Howard insisted Breakfast could sing "Happy Birthday."

"Just listen," Howard had told him the week before. The idiot had squatted before Breakfast, using a carrot as a makeshift baton, singing the birthday song to the pig.

"Happy birthday to you…"

Breakfast would eye the carrot and start whining in her little pig voice. "Grrrrrrr, grrr."

"Can you hear that, Mr. Price?" Howard asked. "She's singing along." He turned and raised the carrot again as he continued the song. "Happy birthday to you…"

"Grrrrrrr, grrr."

"Happy birthday dear Breakfast…"

More caterwauling.

"That's enough, Howard. Give the damn pig that carrot, so she'll shut up."

Buford had no time for such shenanigans today. He had to get the TV working so he could watch the commercials he'd paid for. Folks kept telling him they'd seen the spots, asking him what sort of virtual reality theme park he was opening. He needed to see for himself why everyone assumed Ka Catchers was a damn theme park. Yeah, yeah, he was responsible for Alien Landing and its amusement park, but what he offered the public now had the potential to make people forget all about aliens.

He ordered Howard to take his moron helper over to two chairs facing the TV. "Tell me what you see on the screen."

Howard said, "The TV's not working."

"What do you think I'm doing back here?" Buford snapped. "Come back over here and hold this wire while I look for a jack."

Standing up, he noticed Cracker Jack staring contentedly at the snow on the screen while he clutched an empty caramel corn box, pretending to eat.

Yeah, Ka Catchers hired only the best. This guy made Howard look like a rocket scientist.

"Have you even heard a word I said?" April started in.

156

Before she could get on her soapbox again, he interrupted, "Yes, I've been listening. And no, I don't think the outhouse has any killer fungus. If it did, I'd be sick and so would the commissioner and Grady."

April still paced the room, making wide arcs around Cracker Jack. "Okay, what about Mr. Smith, er, the prince or whatever. He could have been infected and passed it to Micah."

Buford laughed. "That rich guy? You gotta be kidding. He probably lives in a bubble."

He scrounged around in his toolbox but couldn't find a jack, so he headed out the door to see if he could find one in the shed.

Actually, the fungus in the outhouse had crossed his mind, too. Man, the stench was strong and made him gag every time he went near the place. But surely not. Lethal shit only happened in foreign countries, places where little kids wandered around in the streets with flies on their faces. Besides, the crap in the outhouse was a lot newer than the crap in the Roman latrines.

He opened the door to the shed and spotted a corner heaped with rotting cardboard boxes, discarded pop bottles, and shelving lined with old license plates. Where the hell could he find a jack in all this junk? He moved to the first carton on the floor and peeled it open.

Fifteen minutes of rummaging through assorted dusty boxes only yielded one oversized insulator, a handful of broken light bulbs, and an ancient-looking electrical switch box.

He started to sneeze and cough. His throat felt dry, raspy. Must be the dust, or … Naw, he was letting his imagination get the better of him. Brushing off his hands, he pulled a handkerchief from his back pocket and blew his nose. Nothing he needed was in the shed. He kicked the boxes back into the corner and started for the door.

"Buford!" April came running toward him.

What now? That girl just couldn't leave a man in peace.

157

"We have a paying client. Ten grand in cash. He wants to go today. Right now."

Hallelujah. "Well, by God, let him."

"But do you think we should? You know, given..." Her voice trailed away.

"Hell, yes." He pushed past her. "Who is it – somebody local?"

April hurried to catch him. "No. He's not from here. And he says his name is Mr. Smith."

BUFORD shook hands with the latest Mr. Smith, assuring him April could provide advice on everything he needed to know for a safe and enjoyable trip. The guy seemed a bit stiff, not like someone excited about an adventure into the past. Almost military in his bearing, with close, cropped hair and wearing a stoic expression all through the checklist.

When Buford had asked him how he'd heard about Ka Catchers, the guy sidestepped the question without really answering. He'd been just as evasive when asked where he was from. But with cash in hand, it didn't much matter.

Buford ignored the frosty glares from April during her interview with the client. Once Mr. Smith was on his way, she continued to give her boss the cold shoulder. Buford couldn't decide if she was pissed about keeping the outhouse operational or if she was miffed that he wanted her to stay and monitor the client instead of visiting Micah at the hospital.

He suggested they alternate the job of checking the outhouse every fifteen minutes. April sulked, but she did go out when it was her turn. The rest of the time, she texted messages to Micah. No skin off his butt; right now he needed to get the TV fixed.

"Move out of the way, Howard. What are you doing back there?" Buford boomed.

"Just looking."

The screen changed from snow to a sharp image of a CNN anchor delivering the latest world news.

"How the hell did you do that?"

Howard grinned and held up a wire. "I accidentally pulled this off."

Buford picked up the remote and settled into the couch. Howard and Breakfast sat down beside him.

At the same time, Cracker Jack migrated into the chair next to the TV, facing them. Kind of gave Buford the creeps, the way he stared back, his greasy orange hair plastered to his head like a cap. Jeez, the guy needed a shower. The stench drifted clear across the room.

The anchor on the screen began to talk about the global economy. In Buford's mind, the best way to fix things was to go out and spend more money. Not him, of course, his pockets were nearly empty from lack of business. But other people should pitch in. Why, if he had just two more paying customers this week, he might consider renewing his membership in the local chamber. Lots of folks in that organization could benefit from his keen entrepreneurial savvy. On the other hand, might be safer to let his bank account build up a bit more and then decide how to share the wealth, so to speak. After all, wealth needed to come around before it could go around.

The TV screen switched to a new story. Politics, always more politics. The network station ran a clip of some senator talking about illegal aliens. Buford considered himself as patriotic as the next American, but who could blame a guy for taking advantage of some low-cost laborers doing jobs nobody else wanted to. He seemed to recall even Grady had used three seasonal workers the previous summer as hired hands. 'Course, those three turned out to be pretty shifty. More so than the type Buford would have considered. They'd given Perry's visiting niece some trouble, but that gal had showed spunk. Must have sent them scrambling back where they belonged. He never did have a chance to take her out before she left town. When Ka Catchers was on the map, he'd look her up. Nothing turned women's heads more than a prosperous up-and-coming businessman.

April walked into the main room, cell in hand and fingers busy texting. Buford would have to rethink his own labor situation. With business so slow, he might have to let Micah go. Maybe Perry, too. The man had too many ideas of his own anyway, and Buford didn't seem to intimidate him much. April could start doing the ghost tours.

On the news, an attractive blond woman droned on about some international crisis.

He was pretty sure Perry would insist on a Day Trip. Wasn't a very fair trade since he'd only given a few …

"…the Prince of Yadim…"

The words jarred Buford from his thoughts, and he jerked his head again toward the TV.

".. missing from his Denver penthouse since last Tuesday, according to a palace spokesperson."

A picture of the prince replaced the anchor on the screen while she continued to talk. He opened his mouth to holler at April to come watch, but she jumped in front of the TV, blocking his view.

"Your turn, Buford, to check the outhouse."

"In a minute. Look at this." He craned his head to see past April and motioned her to move out of the way.

"C'mon, we had a deal." She blocked his view even more.

"April, move!"

Clearly reluctant, she retreated one step to the side, but enough for Buford to see the image of their no-show client with an overlay of his name, *Abdul-Qadir, prince of the House of Al Shamie.*

"Hey, there's our Mr. Smith," Buford said.

The prince wore a smug expression of superiority, a row of awards and decorations pinned to his uniform. Atop his head sat a military-style orange beret.

"Ha! Know who he looks like?" Buford guffawed. But then his eyes traveled back and forth between the screen and Cracker Jack. The color drained from his face.

April reached down, snatched the remote from his fingers, and muted the voice. "I can explain."

APRIL couldn't take her eyes off the little blue vein that pulsed on Buford's temple. It grew larger by the minute and started to turn purple. Foamy specks of spittle gathered at the corners of his mouth and sprayed her every time he spoke.

"I can't believe it!" he shouted.

Luckily, she'd ushered both Howard and Cracker Jack outside before she told Buford. It would have scared the bejeezus out of both them the way he reacted. Kicking, cursing, sweating – he went through the whole gamut of hysteria for a man who'd just learned law enforcement agencies of the entire world could start breathing down his neck at any moment.

Breakfast weaved in and out between his legs as he stomped from one end of the room to the other. Marching to the TV table, he pounded the top of the set, the force cracking the monitor and toppling the set onto the floor. The pig scurried out of harm's way to cower in the corner.

April had never seen this side of Buford. She worried he might have a stroke. "Calm down. Things have worked out so far. No one's recognized him."

"But they will. I did." He sidestepped the broken television and stopped in the middle of the room. "We have to get rid of him. Get him off the premises. Maybe buy him a one-way bus ticket to Antarctica."

161

That'd been her first thought, too, when the Feds had shown up. But Micah wouldn't hear of it. His rationale had jolted her back to reality and their responsibility toward Mr. Smith-Cracker Jack-Abdul-Qadir.

"Don't be ridiculous. He can't take care of himself, and it's our fault he ended up a zombie."

"We didn't force him to take a Day Trip. He knew the risks."

April walked to the desk and retrieved a contract. She shoved it in Buford's face. "Where on this little piece of paper does it mention this kind of risk?"

Buford slapped it away.

"It doesn't matter whose fault it is. We'd do better by putting our heads together to solve this problem," she said.

Buford's face had taken on a bluish-white cast. He still looked like he was about to blow a gasket or pass out or both.

"Breathe, Buford. Breathe!" April commanded. She backed him up to the couch and gave him a push.

"Were you and Micah *ever* going to tell me?"

In truth, they'd pretty much decided not to. "Of course we were! We just wanted to wait. You know, Cracker, I mean Mr. Smith, could come back. We don't understand how all this stuff works."

Of course, Mr. Smith would never come back. But Buford didn't need to know that right now. What had she and Micah planned to do with him? Other than the immediate solution of disguising him, they never had a chance to discuss it in detail before Micah collapsed in the Lazy S. If only he could be here now to back her up. If only he could be here at all, instead lying in a hospital bed.

"Okay, okay, we've got to think of something fast." Buford's eyes roved the room as though looking for a magic answer. "His hair has to turn blue – or maybe we'll shave his head. Where is he, anyway?"

"I took him and Howard outside so they wouldn't have to see what hysterics look like."

Buford wiped the spit from his mouth and gave the approaching pig a shove with his foot. "Well, get Cracker Jack back in here."

Walking out the Welcome Center's back door, April looked at the empty spot by the shed she'd last left them. They had to be around somewhere. She pulled out her cell phone and dialed Micah's hospital room while she walked around the house and barn. It only rang once.

"Hello?"

"Hey, Micah, your voice sounds a lot stronger."

He coughed. "Yeah, I think I feel better. They might let me out tomorrow while we wait for the tests to come back."

From behind her, April heard Buford yelling and swearing.

"I can't talk much right now," she told Micah, "but Buford knows about Cracker Jack. Who he is really is."

She briefly filled him in on the past twenty minutes of chaos. Between his coughing fits, she could make out what sounded like, "oh shit."

"Don't worry. I'll take care of it. You just take care of *you*. Call ya later." She snapped the phone shut and continued her search for Howard and Cracker Jack.

A ruckus in one of the old buildings behind the barn caught her attention. She swung around and backtracked to a dilapidated chicken coop. When she first opened the door, she couldn't see much. Dust and cobwebs covered the old windows, and the door itself only opened enough for her to squeeze through.

That's when she saw them.

"I told him not to do it, April, but he wouldn't listen," Howard wailed.

She crouched and peered a little closer at the orange-haired man sitting on the old roosting boxes. Feathers trailed from his jaw, and he crunched on something.

"What the . . .?" she half whispered.

"He ate a pigeon! I told him not to, but he did anyway." Howard started weaving back and forth, sobbing and sniffing.

Great. She now had on her hands two hysterical men, one invalid, and one serious carnivore.

"How'd he catch it?" April asked, hardly believing Cracker Jack was coordinated enough to snare a bird.

"It was already dead."

If this had been any other time, April might have been horrified. But this week, it simply seemed like the normal course of events.

She sighed. "C'mon, you guys. Buford wants us. But don't go into the Welcome Center before I hose off Cracker Jack."

AS SOON as the three of them walked through the door, Buford pulled the dripping Cracker Jack upstairs to the dressing room. April knew what he intended to do: outfit their pigeon-eater in a disguise more effective than orange hair.

She watched while Cracker Jack became Christopher Columbus, Napoleon Bonaparte, and Betsy Ross. Buford worked frantically, not always matching costume pieces with the correct person or period. Cracker Jack stared at himself in the full-length mirror with each new wig or pair of pantaloons. Then he would casually pull or tear everything off.

"He's not going to keep that stuff on, you know," April said.

Next, Buford pasted a Fu Manchu mustache to his face. Cracker picked up the trailing whiskers and put them in his mouth.

"This is impossible!" Buford threw his hands in the air and kicked a Geronimo wig across the floor. Howard shrank against the wall like a whipped dog.

April picked up the wig and began to stuff it in a box when she noticed Cracker Jack reaching for it. First feathers, then hair. This man must've needed some fiber in his diet.

"I don't think so," she told their almost-zombie, moving the box away.

Howard stood. "He must like that one."

Cracker Jack continued to stretch his arms at the box. She looked at Buford and he shrugged. Pulling the black braided wig back out of the box, she handed it to Cracker Jack. At first, she thought he was going to eat it, but he gaped at the hair, poking his fingers through the plaits. Then he plopped it on his head.

"See?" Howard exclaimed. "He likes it! Want to dress me up, too?"

April shook her head. "Not today, Howard." Sometimes he surprised her with his good memory, and she didn't want him to mention the disguise to anyone. Best she got him out of the dressing room. "Did you finish pulling those weeds by the driveway?"

Howard grinned and started toward the stairs. "Gonna right now!" He skipped down and she heard the outside door bang shut.

She stepped back and looked at their new Geronimo. His khaki pants had become torn and his shirt was stained with god-knows-what. Where his shoes had disappeared to, she didn't know. He sure looked like some sort of bum, or a –

An idea struck her. She pushed past Buford and rummaged around the costume trunk until she found a yellow bandana. Next she ran downstairs, returning with a black marker pen. Folding the cloth into a strip, she drew peace signs between the folds.

While Cracker Jack still stared at his new image in the mirror, she dropped the bandana over his forehead and tied it at the back.

Buford said, "You're making him look like some kind of hippy."

165

She smiled. "Exactly. And what do hippies do?"

"Live off welfare?"

"Drugs! They do drugs! It makes them stupid." *Like you are right now, Buford.* "Think about it. Why can't the hippy Cracker Jack answer a simple question?"

She finally saw a signs of understanding spread across his face.

"Because he's our no-good hippy employee always high on the marijuana?"

"You're brilliant, Buford," she said over her shoulder as she plucked a garish vest from one of the hangers. Hopefully, Cracker Jack would like it, too. April pulled his arms through the garment and stood back to admire her creativity. Yep, straight off a corner in Haight-Ashbury.

Once again the door to the Welcome Center door banged, and she figured Howard had finished his chore. Instead, a semi-familiar voice wafted up from the bottom of the staircase.

"Excuse me. Anyone up there?"

It was Mr. Smith Number Two. Oh, God, they had forgotten all about him!

CHAPTER EIGHT

"I found my own way out of the outhouse," Smith Two said.

Relief washed over April. Their newest client had returned unscathed, judging from his composure. Of course, he still seemed a bit dazed from the experience – everyone did. But he appeared in control, just as aloof as he'd been before the Day Trip. He didn't seem disturbed that no one had greeted him when he stepped out of The Time Portal. That was sloppy on Ka Catchers' part. The risks were high enough that they needed to remain on hand with every return.

"We didn't expect you to be back so quickly," April said. "We hope it wasn't too disorienting."

She looked to Buford for support, but he wasn't there. She'd thought he was right behind her.

Then he came clomping down the stairs alone. She wondered what he'd done with Cracker Jack, but he smiled with confidence. "Welcome back, Mr. Smith. Did you have an enjoyable Day Trip?"

"Appeared authentic enough."

The new Smith had told April beforehand he wanted to visit the McCarthy Era and sit in on some of the trials. Seemed safe enough to her. All the paranoia during the investigations kept people in line, which minimized bodily risk to their client.

"But I'm more interested in how your time machine works," Smith Two said.

"Trade secret," Buford replied.

He'd dropped into the same voice April heard him use when the commissioner came back. He'd told her he wanted to sound mysterious. She thought it made him sound like he sold used cars.

"I *can* tell you," Buford continued, "it might have something to do with the ley lines intersecting over Silverville."

"Ley lines," Smith Two repeated. "I hardly see how magnetic anomalies can generate sufficient energy to account for a retrograde time dilation."

Buford gave him a blank stare.

"Einstein's Special Theory of Relativity suggests gravity is the most important component of altering time, but there seems to be no fluctuations of that sort in this region. Certainly, none that could interfere with the space-time continuum."

"Un huh." Stooping to pet the pig, Buford shot April a glance that seemed to say, *Can you get this guy out of here?*

"Quantum physics, of course, allows for nonlocality of associated particles, what Einstein called 'spooky action at a distance,' but nothing in the literature refers to such operations occurring at different coordinates in time."

A muted rapping sound came from the second floor. All three looked at the top of the stairs.

Buford placed a foot on the first step. "Well, time to feed the other pig. Have a good day, Mr. Smith. Y'all come back, now." He disappeared up the stairs, leaving April alone to respond.

Only, she wasn't sure what the question was. All they knew was that weird stuff happened in Silverville. And when combined with an unknown fungus, things got even weirder.

Time to think on her feet. "Mr. Smith, have you ever heard of the Juanabee Theory of Displacement?" She hadn't either, but it sounded good. "It relates to the fact that we're sitting on an Indian burial ground. According to studies from the ..., uh, the" – she faked a sneeze to swallow her word – "Institute ..."

"Excuse me, did you say the 'Cashew Institute'?"

"Ah, yes, that's it. Well anyway, this institute found out that time distorts around Indian burial grounds. Some folks think it's caused by shamanic influences." She started to sweat. She couldn't think of what to say next. "When I was little girl, my parents lived in Uruguay and –"

"You have no idea how this works, do you?"

"Most people don't know how sausage is made either, but everyone eats it anyway." She could've slapped herself in the head for letting a stupid thing like that fly out of her mouth.

"Well, thank you miss ...?

"Schauers."

He pulled a pen and pad from his pocket. "How do you spell that?"

PERRY poured milk on his cereal, nodding at Lela's concerns.

"It'll be fine, Poopsie." For years, he'd tried to find a "P" name that suited his wife. All the Pantiwyckes held the initials PP, with the exception of his wife, who went by her original name. But it was a Pantiwycke tradition, and he hadn't given up trying out assorted terms of endearment.

"Quit it, Perry. I'm not a Poopsie." She handed him a bowl of sugar. "I wish you'd listen to me. Time travel is unnatural, and going into the future is just plain stupid."

Lela had served as the conservative – and maybe sensible – anchor in their relationship. But where was the fun in sensible? Before he'd married her a few years back, Perry had spent much of his life roaming the planet in search of exotic escapades. When he was a younger man, he'd fled Bedouins across Tunisia, dived off the shores of Madagascar, and organized numerous expeditions to places unknown. Even more recently, he'd wrangled his way out of risky business with black marketeers – all in the name of adventure. These days, not so much.

Then came Ka Catchers, and the opportunity to get his blood flowing again. Except for that blowhard Buford, he liked the folks he now worked with. April and Micah were just kids, really, but they made him feel young again. And then there was Howard. Sure the guy's mental tricycle had a low tire, but what you saw was what you got, no artifice, no lies. And he and Lela went way back. Perry had to chuckle when, just the other day, Howard called to have Breakfast sing happy birthday to her.

As Perry spooned cereal into his mouth, Lela said, "You're going to do it, aren't you?"

Man, that woman had a persistent streak. He nodded and continued crunching.

"Don't plunge a hundred years into the future. Too much uncertainty. Promise me you'll start with something less dangerous."

He looked up." Like what?"

"Silverville. No more than a year from now."

"But Pineapple, where's the fun in that?" The very fact a century into the future *could* hold danger created some of the appeal. *Where's your sense of adventure, Precious?* The only time he'd seen her take a few risks occurred during the town's curse the year before. Once the spell broke, she lost her taste for the unexpected. But to keep peace, he'd honor her request. This time.

He carried his bowl to the sink and rinsed it out. "Time to go, Pansy."

"You're not leaving this house 'til you promise me."

Pecking her on the cheek, he said, "I promise."

170

WHEN Perry awoke, he felt disoriented. An austere dormitory bedroom with gray-painted cement floors, a simple metal desk with a computer. Next to the door a white lab coat hung on a hook.

He rose from the bed and looked out the single window, seeing uniformed sentries patrolling the fenced-in perimeter of the compound he now found himself in.

Something was wrong. After April had escorted Perry to The Time Portal, he concentrated on the time and place he'd promised Lela. But this couldn't be Silverville, and certainly not just a year in the future.

A knock at the door startled him. A muffled voice followed.

"Dr. Codroy, you're wanted in the main research building."

Perry wondered if the voice was talking to him.

"Dr. Codroy?"

Perry reached for the lab coat, took it off the hook, and examined the badge. The name "Dr. Emmet Codroy" appeared under a photo of a man he didn't recognize. Underneath the name was the designation, "Level A Clearance." He caught sight of himself in a mirror beside the door. Apparently, he *was* Dr. Codroy.

"Yes," Perry said in a raised voice that sounded unfamiliar. "I'll be out in a minute."

He flung on the lab coat, ran his fingers through Codroy's thinning hair, and opened the door, almost colliding with the man standing immediately outside.

Perry took a step back. "Yes?"

"I'm here to escort you, Doctor."

Good thing. Perry had no idea where the research building was.

His companion led him through a barren courtyard and down a new concrete sidewalk. Uniformed men and women hurried past them to destinations unknown.

Where was he?

They passed a gap in the building complex, and he glimpsed the terrain, searching for identifying landmarks. There it stood. The familiar turtle-shaped "S" mountain, the letter marked by whitewashed rocks on the north-facing slope.

That answered his question. This was Silverville after all. But not the one he expected.

An officer wearing braids and stripes approached them. Perry's escort snapped to attention and saluted.

April had prepped him to blend in, but Perry had no idea about the proper protocol. Should he salute, too? Probably not, since he wore a lab coat instead of a uniform. He decided to see if he could get away with only a nod.

The officer saluted the escort and returned Perry's nod. "Dr. Codroy, we're sorry to ask you to come to the lab before your usual shift, but we've had a breakthrough."

A lab? A breakthrough? Gee, he sure wished now he'd opted for the Seventeenth Century aboard Captain Kidd's pirate ship. He knew how to swing from a rope and how to thrust a buccaneer's cutlass. He didn't know beans about being a scientist.

But Perry played the part. "We're on our way now."

"Very good," the officer said, stepping out of the way.

Perry and his chaperon continued a couple more hundred yards down the sidewalk until they arrived at a glass-domed structure with a sign that read, "No Admittance Without Authorization."

His escort stopped at the door, waved, and turned to walk away.

Inside, a guard waited and motioned him toward a retinal scanner mounted next to a steel door. Having seen enough movies with this scenario, he leaned forward and positioned his eye over the scanner lens. A green light blinked on and the door slid open.

On the other side stood a woman next to a desk. Her nametag read "Dr. Rosalee Kreuzer" and displayed the same clearance as his own tag. Smiling broadly, she said, "We may have done it, Emmet."

She took him by the elbow and talked as she led him toward a row of lockers. "Your hunch was right. But don't let me get ahead of myself. Let's suit up first."

She started to strip down to her underwear and threw her clothes in a locker. He followed her cue, hoping he'd locate his own locker. He didn't see any with his name, so he tossed his shirt and trousers on a bench.

She looked down at the heaped clothing. "Aren't you going to stow your stuff?"

He would if he knew where. "Nope, let's get going."

"Wow! You must really be excited."

More like really confused. Evidently, this Codroy guy worked on some highly dangerous – or at least, highly classified – projects. He didn't know how long he could play along until they figured he'd had a mental breakdown or something. The woman walking ahead of him in her underwear looked unfamiliar. He knew everyone in Silverville, and she was no local. And what about this whole compound? It hadn't existed a year ago. Someone or some agency had slapped it together in a hurry. All these questions, and he dared not ask a single one.

At the end of the row of lockers, she stepped through a doorway marked "Women," so Perry entered the one marked "Men." Inside, a stenciled sign told him to remove all clothing before showering. He tugged off his t-shirt, boxers, and socks with big holes worn in both heels. Codroy needed to go shopping.

As soon as he stepped over a six-inch high ceramic-tiled ledge, the showers automatically began to spew a fine mist. It smelled like chemicals and he clamped his eyes shut. Two minutes later, the hissing stopped and he risked a peek. The haze cleared and a blinking sign instructed him to put on the disposable paper garments before entering the Level A hazmat area. *Hazmat?* Leapin' lizards, what had he gotten himself into? But with no underwear, there was no place else he could go.

He searched for a large enough paper suit, including paper booties, from the shelves in the room beyond the showers and put them on. No more signs told him where to go, but the room only had one other door. He stepped through and found Rosalee already pulling on a hazmat suit. Great, he had no idea how these things went on, and he'd lost the opportunity to watch her first.

He reached for the remaining suit. Looked a little more complicated than the diving gear he'd worn off the coast of Madagascar. As far as he could tell, the contraption came with a full face piece, including a self-contained breathing apparatus with an escape cylinder. Accompanying accessories provided boots with steel toes and gloves he guessed were chemically resistant.

"You theory guys can never figure out how to suit up." Rosalee walked over to help him. Once her own headgear was in place, she adjusted his and tested the two-way radio. "Can you hear me okay?"

"Loud and clear."

She turned away from him, grasped and twisted a wheel attached to a heavy door that reminded Perry of a submarine hatch. They both passed through and into a space no larger than some of the cramped elevators he'd known in Paris. She resealed the hatch and waited. The suit seemed to stiffen for a moment and then relaxed against his skin. A change in air pressure? Must be some sort of pressurized room exchanging all the air. Rosalee nodded to him and opened a similar hatch at the far end.

He really didn't want to go through that hatch. But she stood outside the airlock, waiting for him.

A bustling staff who all resembled Michelin Tire men, and probably women, moved from table to table, variously peering through microscopes, adjusting lab centrifuges, or shaking stoppered test tubes. They all paused to look at him.

Perry gave a little wave. Over the radio, he heard cheers.

"That's for you, Emmett," Rosalee's voice said through his radio. She handed him a clipboard with notes and equations. "If you hadn't pinpointed the right recombinant RNA sequence, we wouldn't have identified the lethal agent in the fungus. You were right, all we needed to do was ..." The rest of what she told him was gobble-de-gook. But the last few words of her explanation caught his attention again "... and that's what killed those people who entered the outhouse."

Perry dropped the clipboard. He began to feel sick to his stomach. My God, what had happened over the past year? First, he found this heavily guarded compound, and now he discovered people had died in the outhouse. Who had died – and how many? And just as important, what had killed them? He couldn't ask since Codroy had apparently led this whole project. Did this have something to do with Micah getting sick and winding up in the hospital? But April had told him she planned to pick up the boy this very day. Well, this very day, a year ago. If the outhouse *had* made Micah sick, would it eventually affect everyone else the same way?

Rosalee had said killed, not sick. Were Day Trips the cause? He mentally listed the people who'd taken trips – Micah, Buford, the commissioner, maybe one or two more. And now him. *Were we all dead now?*

Perry needed answers.

ALL THAT morning, Perry had pretended to review notes and reports, hoping his staff understood more than he did. He finally broke away in the early afternoon and rushed back to Codroy's apartment to turn on the computer.

He made his first priority to check the online edition of the Silverville newspaper to see if he could access obituaries. The paper didn't have archives. Next he tried various Internet people-finder databases, plugging in the names of those who'd taken Day Trips. Zero results. It was as if none of them had ever lived. Had someone scrubbed all their records? In fact, he could find no references about Silverville, starting almost one year ago. Like the town had simply ceased to exist.

Lela!

He typed in her name. Nothing. Then he remembered to check for Lela Buzzard instead of Lela Pantiwycke. A couple summers back, she'd decided to reclaim her original identity, and Perry had supported her decision. After all, it was that independent streak of hers that had attracted him to her in the first place.

He tapped that name on the keyboard. His shoulders relaxed when the search engine returned multiple results. A bit surprising, actually. How many Lela Buzzards could there be? But when he clicked on the first entry, the screen displayed a story about a woman who'd moved to Southern California about nine months earlier. No photo accompanied the article, but the woman had taken an active role contesting local zoning ordinances. Perry smiled. Sounded like his Lela. She could never resist the chance to champion a just cause.

However, the story gave no background on how long she'd lived there. Or why she 'd moved in the first place. He returned to the original search results and clicked one after the other. Three links took him to news about the same woman in the same Southern Cal town, but he learned nothing useful. Nowhere did any of the articles mention him. Did that mean he and Lela divorced? Or maybe he was dead.

He felt tempted to search for her number and give her a call, but what would he say? *Hi, Poopsie. Whatcha been up to the last year?* And what if it wasn't his Lela? What if Perry answered the phone when Perry called?

At any rate, his Day Trip would end in a few hours. He'd see his wife that night for supper.

Time to do a bit of reconnoitering to see if any of the old Silverville still existed.

Earlier, he'd noticed a set of car keys with a the signature Mercedes-Benz peace-sign logo on a little table by the door. He took them outside and scanned the parking lot. A Mercedes SUV sat at one end, and an older two-seater sports car nearer his door. Emmet didn't seem the type for speedy wheels. He clicked the key fob, and a short squawk drew his attention to the SUV, which flashed its lights twice.

At least he could go off road if he wanted. No telling how far the perimeter of the restricted military reservation stretched.

He got in the vehicle, started the ignition, and pulled out of the parking lot. It didn't take long to find the only road leading away from the compound. Within a few hundred yards, he came to a sentry shack, and the guard waved him on. Ahead, he made out the silhouette of Silverville three miles away. He'd driven this road many times before – leaving Ka Catchers. Easing the SUV to a stop, Perry got out and surveyed the compound. A huge hangar sat right over the spot where he remembered the outhouse.

Jeepers creepers, Buford's whole place was now a maximum security military installation. This looked worse and worse – people killed in the outhouse, Ka Catchers under government jurisdiction, no record of him and the people he worked with anywhere. A strong feeling of numinous dread curdled in his guts. He climbed back into the SUV and headed to town.

Near the city limits, he passed Alien Landing theme park, but no sign stood over the entrance. He could see the amusement rides, all motionless. Looked like no one had visited in a while. Few cars met him on the way into town, and all the passengers wore uniforms. On Main Street, only a handful of the store fronts seemed open for business and only a few shoppers strolled the sidewalks – no one he recognized. Downtown didn't resemble its former self, no longer the bustling business district he'd seen just the day before with Lela. Boards covered the door of Price's Gun Shop, and combat boots now sat in the window displays of Liverless's t-shirt shop. A military surplus store? At least the Lazy S Diner remained open, but he began to doubt he'd know anyone inside.

On impulse, he steered toward his neighborhood. The Fine Funeral Home came into view. Quiet, but then, that building usually looked quiet unless Denton had business at the time. The further he got from downtown, the more disrepair he saw among the homes on either side of the street. Some even looked abandoned – fences sagging, weeds growing in what had once been manicured, showcase lawns.

By the time he arrived at his house, Perry no longer held any illusions of what he would find. He slowed the Mercedes so he could take a good look. As he approached, a soldier emerged from the front door and knelt to hug two small children playing in the front yard. Perry's heart sank; this was no longer his home.

He lingered long enough to see the soldier crawl into a Jeep parked in front of the garage. The soldier drove past him and waved.

Perry pulled around the corner and stopped, dropping his head against the steering wheel. What had happened to his world?

He sat in a daze for several minutes, pondering what to do next. There had to be records somewhere that explained all these changes. It couldn't have happened overnight, and the townspeople would have put up a fight. On the chance the library might still be operating, he put the SUV into gear and pointed it in that direction.

Six blocks later, he parked in front of the red stone building and walked up the steps to the entrance. He opened the door. The inside still looked the same. In place of Mrs. Brumbelow sat a man wearing a starched shirt and khaki pants.

"Afternoon, Dr. Codroy," the new librarian said. "Need help with anything?"

Perry started, but then shifted back into character. "I'm here to look through back issues of the local paper."

The man rose. "Still researching the outhouse?"

"Yes, trying to tie up some loose ends."

Perry knew where the library kept the old newspapers, but he had no idea if Codroy did.

The librarian didn't offer any directions. "Just let me know if you need any help."

Apparently, Codroy knew his way around after all.

Perry nodded and headed down to the basement. He browsed the shelves of folders containing bundles of old newspapers until he found the collection from one year ago. Taking the folder to a table, he thumbed through the pages. Nothing caught his attention at first. Then he saw the headline: "Feds to seize Silverville." The banner subhead announced, "Everyone to relocate in sixty days." He checked the date and reread it again. Only two weeks away – in Perry's own timeline.

He skimmed the article beneath. A statement from a Col. Heller explained how Silverville's strategic location had become essential to national security interests, necessitating the evacuation.

Holy Schmoly, he couldn't believe it. His Silverville was about to disappear. But why? The article was ambiguous and didn't offer any details, certainly no explanations that made any sense. He flipped through pages of the subsequent issues, finding scores of angry letters to the editor from the townspeople. Many of them were by Lela. Piecing the story together, Perry learned the town had tried in vain to block the government take-over. The headline in the final issue read, "Silverville says good-bye."

He thumbed the pages, searching for information he'd missed. One of them flipped open to the obituaries printed three weeks after the first headline. He almost moved past it until he saw a face he recognized. Micah's.

He searched later obits and found ones for Grady O'Grady, Buford, April, and the county commissioner. He gasped when he found his own.

Everyone who'd taken a Day Trip had died.

THE WHOLE group looked stunned. No one had interrupted Perry's account of his Day Trip, but the reaction on each of the faces of the other Ka Catcher team members was different. Buford looked pissed, Micah kept his eyes to the ground, Howard wiped tears from his cheeks, and Cracker Jack the Hippie sucked on the end of one braid.

April felt a rush of panic that left her speechless, at first. Perry's version of the future seemed unbelievable.

"I even went out to the cemetery to check for headstones," Perry said. "After I found mine and Buford's, I quit looking."

"The government can't just take over my property," Buford blustered. "I'll sue!"

April replied, "It really won't matter. You'll be dead in a few weeks."

"The hell I will!"

Perry shook his head. "I'm afraid you will be. It's the fungus, and it's going to kill everyone who spends time inside the outhouse."

"We don't know that for sure." Buford's voice grew louder with every comment. "The future hasn't happened yet. How do we know your version is the right one?"

Micah started to cough. April hadn't wanted to bring him over to Ka Catchers straight from the hospital, but he insisted once he found out Perry had travelled forward in time instead of backwards. All the way there, he'd kept muttering, "I have to know, I have to know." She'd assumed Micah's obsession was because of the bad news he'd gotten from the lab tests. But those test results also answered the questions they all had.

"We have proof Perry's version is right, Buford," April said. She glanced over at Micah, who nodded for her to continue. "Micah has been diagnosed with" – she faltered, having trouble saying the words aloud – "with an incurable respiratory disease. It's fungal, unknown. And … it's fatal."

She broke down sobbing. No one spoke until she regained her composure. "He's only got a few months."

"Actually, just a few weeks," Perry corrected. He flashed an apologetic grimace at Micah. "Sorry, pal."

And if Perry's Day Trip was right, the rest of them would be dead soon, too. Yet all April could think about was Micah. He would be the first. And they probably wouldn't get to go to that drive-in movie. Or hold hands walking down the street. Or watch the sunrise after a romantic night of … She couldn't let her mind go there now.

It all seemed so unfair.

"What I can't figure out," Perry said, "is how the Feds got wind of us in the first place."

Buford scooted forward in his chair. "Our advertising."

"That can't be it, Buford," April said. "Everybody thought Day Trips were a simulation."

Micah interrupted, moaning. "This is all my fault."

"No!" April said. "You couldn't have known how dangerous the fungus was."

"Not the fungus." He tried to take a deep breath, but his chest rattled. "I mean the takeover."

That got everybody's attention.

Micah continued, "It was after Cracker Jack."

"Cracker Jack? Did he take a Day Trip, too?" Perry asked.

"Long story," April told him, "but short answer, yes."

"I'd seen his name in the obituaries, but figured he'd overdosed on drugs."

April turned back to Micah. "So what about Cracker Jack?"

"I called the Feds after what happened to him. I knew then we were out of our league. This needs more research, and somebody else should be in charge, somebody who can figure out the biology and physics behind The Time Portal."

April knew Micah had always been uncomfortable with commercializing the outhouse, but she was taken aback by his actions. "Why didn't you talk to me first?"

"I did. I talked to you all. We don't have any business messing around with time travel. Maybe Brother Martin's group was right. It's outside the laws of God."

"When did you get religion? Besides, you used the outhouse first." Buford's tone was accusing, angry. "And kept it to yourself, too."

"I was wrong. Buford, what we were *doing* was wrong. This shouldn't be a money-making scheme. It's too important. And the right people needed to run the show." Micah slumped back into the couch. He clearly didn't have much energy left.

"But the Feds!" Buford whispered, as though they were lurking outside or had bugged the Welcome Center.

"Okay, yeah, maybe they know about us already," April said. In fact, the nerdy guy who'd Day-Tripped two days ago was probably a plant from ... whom? The Men in Black? That made them part of the government, and everything took time, paperwork, rubber stamps. "At least we're still in control, but we have to do something to *stay* in control."

Perry threw up his hands. "Not sure we have many options."

April stood and faced the other team members. "Of course we do. We have a time machine."

"For now," Perry said.

A DAY later the Ka Catchers group reconvened at the Welcome Center. Each had the task of brainstorming a plan for changing the past – a solution that would stop the takeover and avoid the subsequent deaths.

So far, no one had come forth with a foolproof scenario. An idea had continued to swirl around April's head since the day before, and she wondered how popular it would be. Up to this point, she'd decided to keep it to herself, waiting to see if one of the others came up with something a little less radical.

Perry squinted at the sun beaming through one of the windows and finally broke the silence. "Not sure we can change the future. I've seen it. Know what it holds."

"That's only if there's one future," April said. She didn't expect to share her thoughts so soon, but Perry provided the perfect segue. "I've read that there are probably multiple universes with multiple timelines. Each contains an outcome of all possible scenarios."

"That's right," Micah said, reclining against the couch pillows. "They're sometimes called 'parallel dimensions,' or 'alternative timelines.' Not only is it a theory of physics but both Hindi and Buddhist texts hint at the possibility."

Buford aimed a not-so-gentle shove at Breakfast with the flat of his foot. "Oh *please*, don't tell me you've bought into her crazy stories."

Huh. So Buford didn't believe her this time either. He'd even doubted her when she'd told him about Micah's collapse in the Lazy S. Could be her own fault after spewing tales about the Uruguayan Worm Syndrome and her Russian spy parents. For future reference, maybe she'd tone it down some. Or not.

"Hey, I'm dead serious," she argued. "This isn't exactly a new idea. Scientists have been kicking it around for more than fifty years."

Buford laughed, pulled himself up from his chair and headed to the kitchenette.

April followed right on his heels, talking loud enough for everyone to hear. "Check it out on the Internet. The theory is these universes are all related to ours and they branch off. Wars could have different outcomes, extinct species could exist – the possibilities are endless."

A grunt from Buford. "Yeah, yeah. Good one, April."

She turned to the others with a look of exasperation.

"I think I've heard that theory on TV," Perry said.

Everyone else nodded, even Cracker Jack, although April figured he was only copying them.

"So what are you getting at?" Perry asked.

"We burn down the outhouse. Burn it completely."

April could almost feel the electricity in the room. All eyes fell on her. Micah nodded. She knew he understood her plan.

"Over my dead body!" Buford thundered.

"That won't be difficult, considering your future," Perry said in a calm voice. "Keep talking, April. What do you have in mind, and how will burning the outhouse prevent your death and everyone else's? Except for Howard, we've all been in there."

Smiling, she started to explain, "I mean burning it down in the past. It'll change our future – create an alternative universe, if you will, by sending one of us back before Micah even stumbled on The Time Portal. Whoever draws the short straw travels to an earlier time and sets fire to the outhouse."

The idea seemed to set *Buford* on fire. "This is ridiculous! Whoever gets stuck with that job can never come back."

"And poof! We create a parallel universe where no one dies and the Feds don't take Silverville," Micah offered.

Buford circled the room several times, probably trying to digest the whole notion. He stopped. "Hey, why don't we go into the future and bring back the cure?"

Perry shook his head. "We can't *bring* anything back. Besides, what I saw a year from now was work done by lots of teams, lots of research scientists funded by some serious government resources. No way one person could remember all the details – assuming someone could even get access again. It was a fluke I Day-Tripped as the head of the project."

Perry paused to let the idea sink in before continuing. "I think April's right. We need to go into the past to create a parallel universe and solve this problem."

"But after that, would we be . . . *us*?" Buford asked.

"Us in another universe, I suppose." April looked at Micah. The dark circles under his eyes contrasted with his pale face. They had to act, and soon. At this point she didn't care what version of themselves would live in an alternative future. One where Micah and the rest of them didn't die.

Buford appeared both confused and alarmed. "Well, would we remember any of this?"

"No, not if the theory is correct." Micah answered.

"And the consciousness of the person who goes back?" Perry asked.

Micah bit his lip. "I don't think anybody could possibly know that. My guess is, if it's an alternative universe, the Ba of the traveler doesn't exist once the outhouse is gone. Everything would reset to zero from the moment it's torched."

185

"I don't know." Buford settled back into his chair. Breakfast wandered back within his reach, and his hand dropped absently to stroke her snout. "I just don't know."

"Buford," Perry said in a low, confidential tone, "it would be a chance to reset all the mistakes you've made with Ka Catchers. Ya gotta admit, it's turning out to be another one of your follies."

"Hey!" Buford stroked Breakfast harder, but the pig seemed to like it and nuzzled against his leg.

"You know what I mean. Look, this operation isn't exactly rolling in dough. And all those expenses – the remodeling, the limo, the money you've laid out for all the promo."

Buford nodded, a look of defeat spreading over his face.

Not to mention the problem of Cracker Jack, April thought then said aloud, "It's up to us to reset the past so we can take control of our future."

"There's no guarantee it'll work," Buford snapped. "Look what happened to me on my Day Trip. Came back as a little kid and couldn't even buy a lottery ticket, let alone burn down an outhouse."

A knock at the door interrupted their conversation. April ran to the window and looked at the driveway. She craned her neck against the pane to get a clear view of the intruder at the entrance. She gasped.

"There's a black sedan in the driveway. And four men wearing black suits at the front door."

"And so it begins," Perry said.

CHAPTER NINE

Mr. Smith Two, who turned out to be one of the Feds, looked at his clipboard. "We have confirmation that Ka Catchers LLC, is registered to Buford Cletis Price." He pointed a finger. "That makes you the person in charge."

At that statement, Buford behaved like a cowardly idiot. He stammered and stuttered, pointing at Micah as the person behind the whole idea. It was a total distortion. April could have slapped him the way he was trying to feed Micah to the lions.

"We're not here to arrest anyone. No one has broken any laws that we're aware of."

Except for harboring a missing person.

"Then I don't understand." Buford looked from one to the other of the federal invaders. "Why are you here?"

"We're seizing this property for the sake of national security."

"You can't do that! I'm an American citizen, and I have rights."

"Eminent Domain. It's already done, and you're trespassing."

That might be bullshit. April's natural distrust of the government made her wonder if they were making stuff up as they went along. They called themselves agents of Homeland Security, but she suspected they were Men in Black, covert operators who everyone knew harassed or threatened the public to keep them quiet. They allegedly worked for unknown branches of the government to protect secrets but likely followed their own agenda.

If that's who they were, they had powers unlimited, unmonitored, unsupervised, which put Ka Catchers in deep shit.

Mr. Smith Two continued, "You are all hereby ordered to vacate the premises immediately. You may take nothing with you, and any attempts to disrupt the seizure will result in arrest and federal prosecution."

Sounded like a script he used every day to confiscate property.

"You're making a mistake," April said, doing her best to suppress the panic from her voice. "The fungus is dangerous, lethal, and we've got to –"

"I won't tell you again," Smith Two said.

Perry saluted, a hint of sarcasm in the gesture, and walked out the door.

"But I have a mortgage on this place," Buford whined, as the MIB ushered him out.

"Not our problem," one of the other black-suited men said.

April, with Howard's help, steadied Micah to get him out the door. Cracker Jack stayed behind in the corner, serenely chewing on a piece of Styrofoam.

"You, too, Flower Child," Smith Two told Smith One.

"Howard, I can manage Micah." April jerked her head toward Cracker Jack. "You better help your friend out."

Howard skirted around the new owners of the establishment and tugged at Cracker Jack's arm. A squeal sounded from inside the Welcome Center, and before long Breakfast shuffled outside, too.

The former team members of Ka Catchers stood in the driveway and stared blankly at the building.

Smith Two stepped through the door. "I didn't just mean go outside. I meant get off the property. Now. But don't leave town. We're going to have some questions for you."

As they moved toward their cars – Howard and Cracker Jack toward bicycles – a huge transport vehicle and a number of Jeeps pulled into the driveway. Soldiers piled out and began unloading fence materials from the truck.

"We can't get in there now," Buford said. "We're all gonna die."

APRIL drove slowly to Micah's house. It wasn't far from Ka Catchers – well, now an MIB installation. Neither spoke until she stopped at the curb in front of his house. She couldn't tell if he was exhausted or just mulling over his decision to spill the beans about the outhouse to the Feds.

She placed her hand on his shoulder. "Don't fret over this. You thought you were doing the right thing. They would've found out eventually anyway."

Micah seemed unconvinced. Her new boyfriend had a tendency to overanalyze, and she wasn't sure anything she said could help.

"I'm going to stay with you."

He shook his head. "My mom's due back in about an hour. I just need some sleep."

She started to open her door, planning to help him into the house, but he grabbed her arm.

A weak grin spread across his face. "Hey, I'm not an invalid – at least not yet."

Nodding, April gave in. She leaned over and pecked him on the cheek. "Get some rest. We'll figure out something, okay?" She doubted either of them believed that, but it wouldn't stop her from trying. Micah looked worse than ever. They needed a solution to get to the outhouse, and they needed that solution today.

She watched him go inside, and then she turned the 'Empo around to drive to Perry's house, where they'd all decided to rendezvous. Perry had insisted, saying he had all sorts of "toys" that might come in handy. Everybody knew his reputation as an adventurer in his younger days, and he probably had some spectacular tools hidden away in that garage of his.

Buford's car sat outside by the time she arrived at the Pantiwycke home. She knocked on the kitchen door at the side, but nobody must have heard her. No wonder, with all the shouting. She let herself in.

"Get a grip, Buford," Perry was saying when April slipped into a chair. "You should be proud to have a boy with that much integrity working for you."

"But now I gotta pay for property I can't even set foot on, and it's all his fault!" Buford blared.

"No you won't," April interrupted. "Do we have to keep reminding you? You're going to be dead soon."

"April's right. If the fungus doesn't kill you first, the townspeople probably will after the Feds announce everyone has to evacuate Silverville."

That shut him up – at least for a few moments.

April took advantage of the silence. "Right now the priority is finding a way to break through the fence and get to the outhouse."

"We could drive a car through it," Buford suggested.

"Did you see the electric generators?" April asked. "We'd be fried if we tried."

"Then a bomb?"

"I'm sure nobody would notice a big explosion."

Perry got up and paced the kitchen floor. "Okay, okay. We need some expertise for this operation. I know just the person."

April and Buford asked at the same time, "Who?"

"Lela. She's resourceful. She ran city government for a long time, and helped mastermind strategies to stop all the changes in town when those UFO freaks moved in."

"What?" Buford shrieked. "She tried to block the progress I worked so hard to bring to this town?"

Perry ignored the question. "And she led a resistance group to protect chicken owners during the whole curse episode in Silverville." Both pride and embarrassment colored his words at this last argument. "So I'd say she's had a lot of experience we could use."

April ventured, "But do you want her to know you're about to die?"

Perry grimaced.

She continued, "You'd have to tell her why we're doing this. Why we have to so soon."

The fewer people involved in this, the better, in April's opinion. If word got out prematurely about the evacuation, there'd be mass panic. That was going to happen anyway, of course. Unless they could destroy the outhouse first.

"Do you think they've had time to fence in the whole thing yet?" April asked Perry.

"I doubt it. They'll create an enclosure big enough to cover the whole area. They'll want to be able to see anyone who breaches the perimeter from a ways off."

"Chained link all the way around?" April asked.

"That's what they were pulling out of the truck. But they won't have it electrified until it's done."

"Then we have to act tonight, before they finish."

Perry snapped his fingers. "I've got a shiny new pair of bolt cutters just waiting in my garage."

Buford's jowls began to quiver. "Oh, I can't *tonight*. Bowling league."

Blowing off Buford's excuse, April got up and opened a cupboard door. 'Does Lela keep soda straws?"

"Nope, use spaghetti. It's on the far left."

"How can you think of eating right now?" Buford asked.

Removing the box, she pulled out a single strand of pasta and broke it into three lengths. She walked back to the table, hiding all but the tops in her hand. "Choose."

"Wait a minute, I thought we were going to break in together," Buford said.

She held the pasta under his nose. "We are, but only one is going into the outhouse."

THEY waited until dark and parked their car a good ways from the main entrance. They intended to approach the outhouse diagonally from a quarter mile down the road. Coming in from the back of the little privy would prevent anyone from detecting their clandestine entry. They all wore black.

Perry swiveled in his seat to face April and Buford. "Okay, are we clear on the plans?"

"Yeah," Buford complained. "I'm the Guinea pig."

April shushed him. "We're splitting up once we see the fence. Perry to the left and Buford and me to the right. We check fifty feet of fence to see if it's complete. We meet back in the middle and decide if we have to cut the wire. And don't touch it until Perry uses the tester."

Perry checked his watch. Ten o'clock, time to move. "Everyone turn off their cell phones."

No sooner had he given the order than April's phone chimed.

"Sorry," she said, and flipped it open. "Hello?"

At first she just listened. Then Perry heard her take a deep breath and say, "Oh my God."

Even in the dark, he could tell by the sound of her voice the message was grave.

"I'll be right there." She closed the phone. "That was Micah's mother. He's gone into a coma, and I have to get to the hospital. Turn around and get me back to my car."

"Yeah, you better turn around," Buford added, a glimmer of hope in his tone. "That kid's like a son to me, and I want to go, too."

The plan couldn't unravel now. The timing was too critical to stop.

"No," Perry said. "The best thing we can do for Micah is to finish this. In thirty minutes, this will all be over." That is, if Buford could pull it off.

He gave April's arm a reassuring squeeze, then passed out the night vision goggles and opened his car door. He stepped out and shut it with barely a sound. He heard the other two do the same.

When he switched on the goggles, the landscape lit up in shades of green. He headed left along the fence line, hoping to discover an uncompleted section.

Stepping over brush and rocks, his mind turned to April. Poor kid. He hoped she could concentrate on the job at hand. Bad enough having to work with Buford, but now with his only reliable teammate distracted, their odds didn't look nearly as good. If they screwed up, there'd be no future for any of them.

From the direction of the others, he heard a branch crack, followed by Buford swearing. Good gravy, he'd told that man to move with stealth and be quiet. Ahead, he could tell the fence gave no indication of ending. They'd have to do this the hard way and cut the links. He turned around and retraced his steps.

Minutes later, he regrouped with April and Buford. "Didn't see any breaks," Perry whispered.

The other two shook their heads, reporting the same.

He knelt and opened his knapsack, extracting the electric current tester. He touched the leads to two sections of fence. The meter showed no activity. Now for the follow-up test, the one he always hated. He reached forward and gripped the heavy-gauge wire.

He said, "She's cold."

"Ohhh." Buford sounded disappointed.

Perry felt relief. If it had been hot, they'd have been dead in the water and forced to come up with another plan. Now they could move forward to Phase Two.

Once again he reached into the knapsack, this time to pull out the heavy pair of bolt cutters. He squatted to snap off sections of the interlaced links. Each snap sounded like the loud pop of a gun. But he knew it was his raw nerves amplifying the noise. Snipping as fast as he could, he finally created an opening large enough for even Buford to wriggle past.

Perry crawled through first, and motioned for his teammates to follow. Next he stowed the bolt cutters in the sack. No telling what new locks the Men in Black had installed on the gate leading to The Time Portal.

Like stalking cougars, they moved through the night toward the outhouse. Except for when Buford tripped on a sagebrush and face-planted beside him. Perry reached down and clamped a hand over Buford's mouth to staunch a flow of inevitable curses.

It took less than ten minutes to reach the structure concealing the outhouse. Flattening themselves against the side, they skirted along the wall until they reached the front of the enclosed courtyard.

Perry raised a hand for everyone to stop. Once they approached the gate, they'd all be in full view of any guards stationed nearby. Peeking around the corner, he checked for any activity at the Welcome Center.

Everything seemed quiet. It made him uneasy.

Removing the bolt cutters, he motioned his team to follow. They crouched and trotted single file the last ten feet to the gate.

To Perry's surprise, the gate was unlocked. He pushed it open and they sneaked in.

"What's tha – ... No, Mother of God!" Buford bellowed.

A horrendous, sickening odor filled the courtyard. A skunk must have sprayed Buford. Seconds later, high-intensity lamps flooded the entire area, and Perry heard shouts and footsteps coming from the Welcome Center.

April gagged. "Quick, get him in there!"

Trying to ignore the stench, Perry latched onto Buford's arm and thrust him toward The Time Portal. They dashed across the courtyard toward the fancy façade and Perry kicked the entry open. April sprinted ahead and flung open the outhouse door.

All the while, Buford wailed, "I can't go like this! I can't go in there!"

As Perry shoved him inside, April called, "Remember, think Silverville, six months ago!"

She slammed the door shut.

Within seconds, guards wrestled Perry and April to the ground, slapping cuffs on both.

A burly soldier roughly pulled them to their feet. "You're under arrest for trespassing on a secure federal installation."

Perry saw a smug smile on April's face.

"You're too late," she said.

AS APRIL slammed the door shut on the outhouse, Buford pitched forward and collided with a warm body that his scrabbling motion knocked hard into the wall. Had to be an MIB agent. Outrage surged through Buford. Surely no one would use his facilities for anything other than Day-Tripping.

The commingling odor of skunk, fungus, and outhouse filled his nose. He squeezed his eyes shut and thought about Silverville six months ago.

In a blink, he found himself in the middle of a ballroom floor, dancing with a man in a tuxedo who smelled like alcohol. Buford gave his partner an involuntary shove, and the man staggered a few steps backwards. A roar of laughter filled the space around him.

Someone shouted, "Whatsamatter? Your new hubby getting too fresh before the wedding night?"

Buford turned in a circle to get his bearings. Didn't look like anywhere in Silverville, past or present.

Droves of dressed-up people watched, standing beside tables that crowded one end of the room. The largest table held a huge, layered cake topped with the figurines of a bride and groom. A small orchestra played from the other end of the hall, and bunting draped the ceiling. At the center hung a pair of large Styrofoam wedding bells with the stenciled date July 23 on one bell and 1955 on the other.

Buford glanced down at himself and nearly choked at his long white dress covered with brocade. He reached for his head and felt a lacy veil cascading around his shoulders and down his back.

"My God, I'm a bride!"

The drunk in the tuxedo lurched forward and slurred, "Don't worry, honey, I'll be as gentle as I can tonight."

THREE MIB agents pushed Perry and April into the Silverville County Sheriff's Office. In a defiant move, April jerked her elbow out of the grasp of her captor. *Atta girl, April,* Perry thought. He knew another young woman who had the same spunk, even in handcuffs. His niece Pleasance nearly knocked a copper over with a head butt when the two of them had been arrested inside the Sudan Necropolis digging into one of the Nubian pyramids. They sure could have used her help right now.

A man dressed in a law enforcement uniform rose from the desk. Perry recognized him – but as the city dogcatcher, not the deputy. Guess Arno Aasfresser had weaseled his way up in the world. Lela hated his guts for impounding their dog a couple years back.

"Hold on here. What is all this?" Aasfresser blustered, pushing out his chest.

As if he had the chutzpah to bully anything bigger than a Chihuahua. All those skinny short guys had Napoleon complexes.

"Where's the sheriff?" the head MIB agent demanded.

"Out of town. Won't be back 'til next week."

The agent leading the way flashed credentials at Aasfresser. "We're commandeering your jail."

"Uh, can you do that?" Arno's command of authority shrunk to match his size.

The agent wrestling with April said, "We're government. We can do whatever we want. Show me your containment facilities!"

Arno stepped aside, pointing to a door behind the desk. "We've only got two cells, and one's taken."

The other agents looked to the MIB in charge.

He shrugged. "Throw them both in the same cell."

They marched Perry and April through the door, aiming them at the open jail cell. Once inside, the agents took of their handcuffs and slammed the bars shut.

Agent-In-Charge smiled for the first time. "Don't go anywhere."

After they walked out, April gripped the bars like she was testing them.

Perry sat on the only bed. "What you need is to a cup to rake back and forth."

"I've never been in jail before. Have you?"

A few times. "Shouldn't be for very long if Buford does what he's supposed to."

From the adjoining cell, Perry heard a raspy, drunk voice singing.

"Hang down your head, Tom Dooley
Hang down your head and cry
Hang down your head, Tom Dooley
Poor boy, you're bound to die."

Not exactly the Kingston Trio, and not exactly the song they needed to hear right now.

April plopped down on the hard mattress beside him. "I thought it'd be over already. What do you think the problem is?"

With Buford, lots of things. He'd have to have landed in a body that accommodated the plan. A whole range of possibilities might prevent him from acting. They knew the risks. Jumpin' Jiminy, maybe Buford woke up in a nursing home and Nurse Ratchet wouldn't let him go outside. Maybe he landed back as that same kid and his mom had grounded him. Maybe he had trouble laying his hands on accelerants, or his matches were wet. Whatever the problem, Buford hadn't succeeded yet, or he and April wouldn't be sitting there wondering.

On the other hand, maybe Buford did succeed, splitting the future into an alternative timeline but still leaving them in this one to enjoy the amenities of Arno's jail cell. Oh balderdash, he didn't know *how* this worked.

April interrupted his thoughts with a more immediate concern. "Not much privacy for the toilet." She nodded toward the stainless steel bowl situated three feet from the bed.

"I'll turn my head."

The door leading to the outer office opened, and Arno swaggered in holding his hand over his gun butt.

"Well, well, well. What kind of trouble have we gotten into tonight?" The dog catcher pulled out a baton with his free hand, tapping each bar as he paraded back and forth.

From the next cell, the drunk continued singing in a mournful voice,

> *"This time tomorrow*
> *Reckon where I'll be*
> *Down in some lonesome valley*
> *Hangin' from a white oak tree."*

Arno marched over to their cellmate. "Shut up! You're only in here for disturbing the peace."

The singing turned into slurred complaining.

"You wanna spend an extra night in jail?"

The drunk grumbled and shut up.

Then Arno again turned his attention to Perry and April, a broad and malicious smile creasing his face. "You must be up on pretty serious charges to have the government coming down on you."

He thrust out his lower lip in an exaggerated pout. "Want to tell Deputy Arno all about it?"

"Beat it, pooch police," Perry snapped. "You'd need to be able to count past ten to understand."

"Ooh, touchy, aren't we?"

Perry turned his back and April did the same.

Arno taunted, "Had your dinner yet? If not, I can go heat up your bread and water."

He kept it up a few minutes longer, but when they refused to acknowledge him, he must have gotten bored because he wandered back to the front office.

For the next thirty minutes, Perry and April fretted over what had happened – or rather, hadn't happened. The drunk next door must have fallen asleep, and Arno left them alone, apparently discouraged he couldn't ruffle them.

Their conversation took a maudlin turn when they suspected Buford might have failed in his mission.

"If it turns out we're stuck in this timeline," April asked, "how long do you think they'll hold us?"

Perry had no idea. In a normal situation, they'd likely be released on bail – at least, that was his experience. But under the current circumstances, their captors might hold them longer, maybe even observing them like lab rats once they discovered the lethal consequences of Day-Tripping. "I bet we're out by tomorrow or the next day."

April nodded. "There's lots of stuff I thought I'd get to do before I died. Like all the fun you've had. If the plan fails, and they let us out, what would you do with the time you have left?"

Perry had thought about that already. "Remember when I met you that first time in the library?"

"You were looking at pirate books."

"Thought I might organize one last treasure-hunting expedition with my niece, Pleasance."

"I've never done anything that exciting. Seen lots of places with my folks, but never really did anything."

This was a more somber April than he'd ever seen. No wild stories, no outrageous experiences. For once, she might be telling the truth. "You should come with us."

He thought he saw a spark of excitement behind her yellow cat's eye lenses.

"You serious?"

"Yep. We could use somebody to temper us reckless Pantiwyckes. And I think you'd like my niece."

"Maybe I will. If we get out of here before ..." She turned away from him, and he thought she wiped an eye. Then her tone shifted, sounding more like the old April. "You've done so many things, had so many adventures already. What do you want people to remember about you?"

He grinned. "That Perry had done so many things and had so many adventures. What about you?"

She scrunched up her face in thought. "That underneath her crazy stories, April really was a good person."

A commotion at the front of the building interrupted the conversation. Something was up.

Perry rose and pressed his ear hard into the space between two bars.

April asked, "Can you hear anything?"

"Shhh."

He heard garbled shouts but couldn't make out whose voices spoke beyond the closed door. But he then recoiled at an acrid whiff coming from the other side. "You smell that?"

"It's Buford!" April said, and she pulled out the tail of her shirt to cover her nose.

The door flung open. Buford flew in first, several steps ahead of his jailers.

Arno gagged. "Can't we chain him up outside?"

The same Men in Black stayed just beyond the door. One of them answered, "We hosed him down. What more do you want?"

Arno unlocked the cell door and shoved Buford inside. "Here's somebody to keep you company. Hope you like his cologne." He rushed back to the front and slammed the office door behind him.

At least Arno wasn't likely to bother them much.

April spoke first. "What happened?"

Buford shook like a wet dog, pelting his cellmates with skunky droplets.

"What went wrong?" Perry asked.

"Everything. For starters, there was already a Day Tripper in the outhouse when you shoved me through the door."

"What?!" April looked at Buford in disbelief. "Who would have been in there?"

"A Fed, their butler, their gardener. How the hell should I know?"

201

April slumped onto the bed. "You went on his Day Trip, didn't you?"

Slicking back his hair, Buford replied, "Damn right, just like what happened to you."

"Where did you go?"

Buford's face turned crimson. "Well, it wasn't Silverville, and it wasn't six months ago."

"Then we're screwed."

Buford took a deep breath. "You can sure say that again."

NEXT morning, Arno walked into the cell room plugging his nose. Buford opened one eye. He'd tried to sleep sitting against the wall, but didn't find it very restful. The others kept complaining about the reek. Now that the drunk next door had sobered up, he complained, too.

It wasn't Buford's fault; it was the skunk's, and the MIB for not letting him take a shower.

Arno stepped up to their cell and tossed a bundle of clothing at Buford. "Change into these. Fresh from the thrift shop." He raised his voice. "Look sharp, you losers. You've got a busy day ahead of you. The interrogation team is here."

"Where are they taking us?" Perry asked.

"Nowhere. They brought a torture chamber with them. It's parked right outside."

Stripping down while April turned to face the wall, Buford unwrapped the bundle and found the pants two sizes too small. He couldn't button them, so he left the tails on his hand-me-down shirt hanging out.

Three agents came through the door and pushed Arno out of the way. One unlocked the cell, and the other two cuffed the Ka Catcher team members.

They found themselves escorted out of the building and whisked toward a large mobile trailer parked at the curb.

Torture? Had Arno said *torture chamber*? Buford didn't like the sound of that. Arno was just trying to scare them, that must be it. What an asshole. Stuff like that didn't happen, not in the good old US of A. Nevertheless, Buford's mouth felt dry and his palms sticky.

Behind him, April argued with her guard. "Keep your grubby hands off me! I can tell where we're headed."

What an attitude that girl had. Now was not the time to be sassy or belligerent.

Mounting steps attached to an entrance at one end, Buford stumbled inside and felt hands guiding him down a hall and into a cubicle. As they shoved him in, he saw April and Perry thrust through different doors.

Another Man in Black, or brown rather, sat waiting in the small bare room. His torturer? Short in stature and unremarkable except for bushy eyebrows and a gold cap covering one of his upper front teeth.

Buford scanned the little room. A large mirror hung on one wall, and three chairs and a desk filled most of the space.

"Have a seat, Mr. Price." The interrogator pointed to a chair opposite him. "Would you care for coffee or water?"

Buford dropped into the hard wooden seat a good six inches shorter than his interrogator's. "Coffee, thanks."

The man stood and popped his head out the door, calling, "Some coffee here, please. And bring some of those croissants."

That was more like it. Maybe this wouldn't be so bad after all.

Returning to his seat, the man extended his hand. "I'm Mr. Smith."

Another one? Buford almost started to laugh. Imagination must run short in the government.

Mr. Smith Three continued, "You've had quite the ordeal over the past twelve hours."

"You can say that again."

"Let's see if we can get this straightened out."

About that time, a woman entered with a tray of coffee and croissants. Mr. Smith thanked her and she walked back out. Buford could have sworn he heard the click of a deadbolt. But he sure couldn't hear anything else. The room must have been soundproof.

Smith Three told him to help himself, and Buford did. Designer coffee, strong the way he liked it. The croissant, on the other hand, wicked at the saliva in his mouth. He dunked pastry in his brew, not giving a shit what this guy thought of his manners.

The hot coffee boosted his confidence. "Why the hell am I here?"

The cordial smile of the interrogator disappeared. He tapped a pencil on the desk for a good three minutes. Then he lunged forward just inches from Buford's face. "We want to know why you trespassed onto federal property and entered the outhouse last night."

Leaning backwards, Buford nearly toppled his own chair. He dropped his soggy croissant on the floor, and stammered, "I'm, I'm not saying anything until I call my lawyer."

"This is a matter of national security. You don't have the right to an attorney," Mr. Smith barked. After a moment, he returned to tapping his pencil. His tone became polite once more. "I'm going to ask you again. What were you doing in the outhouse last night?"

Buford panicked. He didn't know how to answer. One minute the guy was the perfect host and the next a pit bull. Maybe he should confess everything.

"If you go in that outhouse, you're gonna die," Buford said.

Smith Three flicked his pencil at Buford. "Are you threatening me?"

"No, you don't know what I mean."

The door opened and a hulking man bolted through. He stopped short and settled into the third chair, glaring.

Smith never took his eyes off Buford. "Maybe you better start explaining what you mean."

The hulking man pulled a roll of tape from his pocket and began wrapping his knuckles.

"This can be pleasant or extremely unpleasant," Smith said.

A warm tickle trailed down the inside of Buford's pants, creating a small, yellow pool under his chair.

Mr. Smith looked at the puddle in disgust. "We're not getting anywhere," he said to the hulking man. "You can leave for now."

Then he turned to Buford. "We're going to take a break and let you think about this. I'll be back in a few minutes."

Relieved his tormenters had left him alone, Buford sopped up the urine from his chair with the napkins that came with the croissants. He dabbed at his pants as he stepped to the mirror. The face looking back needed a shave. Baring his teeth, he realized it'd been twenty-four hours since he'd brushed. He leaned closer to the mirror and picked at a small string of spinach left over from yesterday's lunch.

A MAN with bushy eyebrows and a brown suit entered April's cubicle. Left alone after her initial interrogation, the suspense had been killing her.

"Good morning, Miss Schauers," he said, extending a hand. "I'm Mr. Smith."

Of course you are.

Pleasantries took up the first few minutes, and he offered her coffee and croissants. She declined.

"I've had a little chat with Mr. Price about why the three of you broke into the outhouse last night. He tells me you planned to remove something essential from that structure."

205

He did? The statement confused her. Why would Buford say something like that? Could this guy just be fishing for more information? If that was the case, April could play the game.

"If he's already told you, why ask me?"

"Just verifying what he intended to take."

"Toilet paper, Mr. Smith. Toilet paper. Buford's incontinent." Let him chew on that for a while.

But to her surprise, Mr. Smith nodded his head as if this made sense.

"He couldn't just purchase toilet paper?" he asked.

Think fast, April. "He thinks it's magic paper, like the outhouse. But you already know about The Time Portal."

"Has he shown any signs of instability?"

Now April was in her element. She decided to ratchet the story up a notch. "He's not been the same since he tripped over that pig and hit his head. Buford talks to it, you know. He says the pig tells him things."

"That doesn't explain why you and Mr. Pantiwycke accompanied him last night."

April shrugged. "He was our boss. We were afraid he'd hurt himself or do something stupid."

"What you all did was stupid. Do you realize what your actions could mean for your future?"

She sure as hell did, but she wouldn't explain it to Mr. Smith. That would only make the Men in Black more vigilant, and Ka Catchers still had to find a way to burn down the outhouse.

"WE TRIED to stop him but we couldn't. He was like a crazed madman." Perry had to be careful what he said to Mr. Smith. He understood how interrogations worked. Detectives would go from one interview to the next, trying to piece together clues to build a theme. Then they'd stand back and wait for perpetrators' reactions.

The interrogator tapped his pencil on the desk. "Did he say anything about toilet paper?"

The question threw Perry off. Toilet paper? What was he getting at? Better to stay vague. "Buford fixated on lots of stuff."

"Like what?"

"Everything about the outhouse. You name it."

"Is he obsessive-compulsive about other things, too? Places, people... animals?"

What was Smith trying to get him to say? And why had he brought up animals? Had to be something April had mentioned in the cubicle next door to throw the Men in Black off track. Perry thought hard. The only animal Ka Catchers had was Breakfast. If that's what April had brought up, he'd run with it.

"He has this pig." Perry leaned forward as though speaking in confidence. "And if you ask me, his relationship with it is pretty unnatural..."

"HE'S NOT responsible for his actions anymore," April said. She took a dramatic breath. "Okay, I didn't want to tell you this, but he was trying to commit suicide. I think the pig talked him into it."

"And you were going to help him?" Smith Three asked.

"No! We went along to stop him."

He set his pencil down as the muscles in his jaw relaxed for the first time that day. Looked like her interrogator might have accepted her explanation for now. Along with whatever testimony Perry must have given him.

Smith stood. "You realize you still trespassed on restricted federal property, and you'll have to face the consequences."

April nodded, doing her best to look penitent. Boy, she hoped she had a chance to talk to Perry. They still needed to find a way to get someone into that outhouse.

Smith escorted her out of the cubicle and handed her over to a Woman in Black, who recuffed and led her outside. A moment later, Perry also emerged from the trailer, escorted by his own guard.

The woman said, "Sorry, you and this other gentleman" – she pointed to Perry – "will remain in the local jail for a couple more days. We're making arrangements to transfer you to a secure facility."

"Can we have visitors?" April asked.

The woman's lips scrunched into a small frown for a second, considering the request.

"Or make a phone call? I need to check on a sick friend."

The Woman in Black shook her head. "Sorry, against regulations."

It wasn't what April wanted to hear. She desperately needed to know Micah's condition. But now it seemed impossible. With the way things looked now, she might never see him again unless that outhouse burned.

She glanced around at a disturbance. She spotted Buford across the parking lot, trussed up in a straightjacket while Men in White dragged him screaming toward an unmarked van.

CHAPTER TEN

By now, Lela had accustomed herself to Perry's odd, nocturnal hours. His biorhythms kicked into gear about the time she readied for bed. Theirs had been a whirlwind romance later in life, but they'd at last settled into routines that worked for them both.

Only, Perry seldom stayed up –certainly not out of the house – until the next day, and she'd have expected him to call her, so she wouldn't worry, by the time she rose around five-thirty in the morning.

But Lela *was* worried.

Ever since he'd taken his Day Trip the day before yesterday, he'd acted pensive and withdrawn. She kept asking why. He refused to talk about it.

Then last night he'd told her he had business at Ka Catchers that would keep him away until late evening, oddly vague about the "business" he was up to. He'd kissed her good-bye and told her not to wait up. Good thing. She checked the clock for the umpteenth time. It was now ten-thirty in the morning, and still no word. She tried his cellphone repeatedly, but no answer. Buford didn't answer his cell either.

She snatched up her car keys, deciding to drive out to the operation. Perry had some explaining to do.

As she approached Ka Catchers, she noticed a wire fence around the whole perimeter she didn't recall seeing before. Had Perry and the crew spent the entire night constructing this new addition? She pulled into the driveway, surprised to see strange men in uniform blocking her entrance.

One came to her window. "This is federal property, Ma'am. No admittance unless you have high-security clearance."

"But this is Ka Catchers. My husband works here."

"Not anymore."

Flustered, she argued with the guard. "But where are the people who used to work here?"

"I wouldn't have that information. And if I did, I wouldn't be allowed to divulge it." At that he turned and walked away.

In a daze, she pulled out of the driveway and headed back to town. By the time she reached the city limits, the daze turned into full-fledged panic. Had she slept through a week and Perry hadn't awakened her? No, couldn't be.

This was weird even by Silverville standards.

She'd head straight to the sheriff's office and file a missing person report. But first, she whipped by the convenience store to grab a newspaper and see if it said anything about the startling changes at Ka Catchers.

The headlines on the upper fold stunned her. "Feds to seize Silverville." She read further. The government gave residents sixty days to clear out. The feds claimed the right of eminent domain in the interests of national security. Although the story made no mention of the cause, Lela knew it had to do with Buford's time portal.

A sidebar next to the story quoted Mayor Earl Bob Jackson. "We're disappointed the government felt it had to seize the entire community. They've given us no opportunity to argue our case.

But we're not going down without a fight. We encourage everyone to attend a town meeting scheduled tonight to discuss all available options."

Perry or no Perry, she didn't intend to miss that meeting.

She drove toward the sheriff's office, her stomach churning at the thought of everyone forced out of their homes. For thirty-five years, she'd lived in her cozy, one-story bungalow, first with Schloppy – God rest his soul – and then with Perry. Who did those fed-heads think they were, simply tossing people out on the street? Where did they expect folks to go? Her next-door neighbor was wheelchair-bound, with no kin left. People across the street had eight kids and spent years building additions onto their house. Fawn, the Lazy S waitress, just moved into her new home a few years back. Others folks she knew had lived in town for decades, and their families for generations. And what about all those newcomers who'd moved in after Buford had turned Silverville into a UFO mecca?

Damn that Buford. If she could get her hands on him, she'd wring his neck.

Lela flew past the sheriff's office going fifty miles-per-hour. *Oh! That's right, Perry.* She hit the brakes and squealed to a stop. She reversed direction with a three-point turn and came to a halt at the curb in front of the building.

Newspaper rolled and clinched in her fist, she marched through the door and up to the desk.

"Mornin', Miz Pantiwycke," Arno drawled.

She swung her newspaper bat across the desk and smacked him in the head. Hard.

"What do you know about this evacuation, and what do you plan to do about it?" she demanded.

Arno covered his head with his arms, cringing. "Ow! What was that for?"

"You're our deputy sheriff, and you're supposed to protect our community, you good-for-nothing dog catcher!"

"We can't do nothin' about that," he whined. "The Feds got jurisdiction."

Lela took a deep breath. She should've known this sad excuse for a lawman wouldn't help. She'd warned Carl not to hire him.

"Where's Carl? I need to talk to someone with a backbone."

"Fishin'. Won't be back until the end of the week."

"Okay, but you better be at that meeting tonight." She shook the paper in his face. At that moment she remembered why she was there. *Oh! That's right, Perry.* "I need to fill out a missing person report on Perry."

Arno's expression changed from fear to arrogance. "He ain't missin'. He's in the slammer back there." He jerked a thumb over his shoulder.

As Lela stormed past him, he rose from the protection of the desk, asserting, "I'm not sure I can let you back there."

She raised the paper in his face again. "Just you try to stop me, you little weasel."

He returned to his chair, refusing to meet her glare.

"HOT DAMN! It's good to see your face," Perry called out from between the bars. He'd heard the commotion through the door, recognizing his wife's voice – and Arno's sniveling one. As always, Lela proved a force unto herself, and he'd figured once she knew about his imprisonment there'd be no stopping her.

He was right.

When the MIB had returned them to the Sherriff's Office, the drunk was gone, so they'd placed Perry in that cell and April in their old one. An entire wall now separated the two, but they could still talk through the bars.

Too bad about Buford; he wasn't much help anyway. No matter what he told the Feds now, no one would believe him.

What a stroke of luck both Perry and April focused on the pig, even if the Man in Black tried to play them against each other. But Perry didn't fall for it. He'd gathered just enough info to guess what April told Smith Three.

Problem was, they needed somebody else to go back and burn down that outhouse. They hadn't had much opportunity to come up with an alternative plan, and didn't see how they could recruit outside help with the kibosh on visitors.

But here came Lela, waltzing in through the front door, blowing past Arno. Perry smiled. *That's my girl! And my hero.*

"Perry Pantiwycke, what's going on?" she said, striding up to his cell.

"They threw us in the pokey."

"Who's 'us'?"

Perry tilted his head toward the dividing wall. "Lela, you know April."

A rustling came from April's side as his wife stepped over to peer into the adjoining cell.

Lela backed up so she could see them both. "And just what did you two do to land yourselves in the pokey?"

"Actually, it was Buford, too. Until they hauled him off in a straight jacket."

Perry spent the next fifteen minutes bringing Lela up to speed on the events of the past twelve hours – breaking in, arrested, interrogated, pending incarceration in a "secure facility." 'Course, he left out the part about their imminent deaths.

Not a twitch of an eyebrow or a gasp of surprise from Lela. So typical of her pragmatic personality.

Then April called out from her cell, "You better tell her the rest, before the Feds find out she's here."

Perry cleared his throat. "Oh, yeah, there's one more thing. Every Day Tripper will die in a few weeks."

Finally, a reaction. Lela's face flushed. "You're getting executed?"

"No, it's the time-traveling. I found out from my Day Trip to the future the fungus in the outhouse is lethal. We planned to send Buford back in time to burn it down before any of this happens. That's what we were doing last night."

Lela unfurled and held up the newspaper she carried. "Then you knew about this, too?"

He read the headlines and nodded. The demise of Silverville was starting sooner than he expected. No time to waste.

April shouted, "Are you thinking what I'm thinking, Perry?"

Yes, he suspected he was. To Lela, he said, "You can help us."

Raising her hands to her hips, she asked, "How?"

He drew himself up to the bars and motioned her closer.

LELA arrived early and took a seat near the back while townsfolk filed into Town Hall. They all looked scared, angry, frustrated.

As people sat down, she placed her purse and sweater on the chair next to her. She didn't want to talk to anyone. She only wanted to gather the kind of information that might help her later that night. When Perry and April had explained their solution, she had trouble wrapping her head around the whole past-present-future concept. It seemed to her that once the future was defined, nothing she could do would make a difference.

"Not the case," Perry told her. "Remember when Howard won the lotto? That's not how it really happened – the first time."

"Huh?"

"Before Buford went back in time, he'd read in the newspaper that Earl Bob Jackson won the lottery. So Buford used his Day Trip to finagle the lotto for himself. He screwed up and Howard won instead. That means we can tinker with the outcome of events. At least to some extent. At any rate, we gotta try. It's our only hope."

Lela never could get it; she just had to trust that Perry knew what he was talking about.

Her neighbors with the eight kids tromped down the aisle. They slid into seats toward the front of the room, taking up an entire row. A pair of women sitting directly ahead of her grumbled loud enough for her to hear one complain about the garden she'd spent all summer tending.

"Looks like I won't be even be here to the harvest the peas and onions."

The woman's companion responded, "I know what you mean. My Herbert pulled the engine out of our car to overhaul it. At the rate he works, we won't even be able to get out of town in time."

She spied Grady and Leona O'Grady as they squeezed into two chairs across the room. A momentary twinge of regret gripped her, recalling how Perry had told her Grady, too, had time-traveled. He'd have the same fate as the Ka Catcher team. She'd often felt frustrated at the old rancher, his ornery nature getting in her way more than once as she tried to steer events in their little burg. But he represented part of what made Silverville so special. Not the ley lines, the UFOs, the curses. It was the people who made her proud to be a citizen of their town.

The hall echoed with grumblings of unhappy people as more and more crowded into the space. She felt a sense of pride swelling inside her to see so many show up. She'd watched this place grow for years, pulling together to suffer through bad times and celebrate the good. Her community never hesitated to voice different opinions. They shouted and cursed at each other until somebody came up with a workable resolution.

This resolution they'd never know, and she couldn't reveal it.

215

A gavel sounded and Mayor Earl Bob Jackson called the meeting to order, but it took several minutes for him to get everyone settled down. He really had his hands full this time, and she didn't envy him his job right now. As former mayor herself, she understood how difficult the next hour would be as he tried to keep everyone calm and the meeting productive. Lela shifted in her chair to see between the two women sitting in front of her.

"Meeting to order!" Earl Bob shouted, rapping the gavel three more times.

The din died down as everyone settled into their seats to turn attention to the mayor.

"You all know why we're here," he began.

Someone from the audience shouted, "No, we don't. Why are we being forced from our homes?"

Complaints erupted across the hall, and Earl Bob raised a hand to silence everyone. "The government hasn't explained their reasons. At this point, I don't know much more than what we've all read in the paper."

"Why would they take a sudden interest in Silverville?" another voice asked.

"That's what we aim to find out. I've organized a delegation to meet with federal officials to get some answers. In the meantime, if this moves forward – and I hope it doesn't – we've got to decide how to make this as painless as possible."

"I ain't moving," a voice from the middle of the crowd said.

Earl Bob strained to locate the speaker. "Grady, was that you?"

The old rancher stood and limped toward the raised platform up front. Lela waited for the tirade sure to follow. No one ever told Grady what to do and got away with it. If the Feds tried to forcibly to remove him from his family homestead, the confrontation would likely end up in a shootout. If he lived that long.

"I reckon we can blame this situation on Buford Price."

216

Members of the crowd exchanged glances, seemingly confused by the accusation.

Grady continued, "And I'll tell you why. That Ka Catchers' place is fenced up now. Guards swarming all over the place. I seen it myself comin' to the meeting tonight. It's that time-travel foolishness."

Another eruption of chatter spread through the room.

The mayor asked, "Are you trying to tell us the security issue is because of Buford's new business?"

"Yep. Why else would they have that place corralled off like a hidey-hole for stolen horses?"

Lela cringed. Once again, Buford managed to bring the wrath of the community down on his head. First with his failed ski resort, which everyone called Buford's Folly and nearly bankrupted the town from tax levies. Second, with his scheme to turn Silverville into a UFO sideshow. She'd been mayor herself during that escapade, and she saw the town struggle with increased population and all the infrastructure that came with the growth. Changed the flavor of the community in ways that still resonated with many of the town's original residents. But nothing topped this.

"Where is that son-of-bitch anyway?" an angry man bellowed.

"Probably sunning himself on some beach in the Bahamas!"

More likely squatting in a padded room eating with plastic spoons.

The same angry man said, "I bet he's sitting at Ka Catchers right now making a deal with the government. Let's go get him, boys!"

A dozen men jumped to their feet and headed for the door.

Grady shouted, "Don't let yer britches get afire! You'll never git in. Them soldiers got bigger guns than you."

The vigilante group paused, waiting for Grady to continue. He didn't. Just walked back to his chair.

In Lela's mind, this gathering had turned into a bust. The bulk of it consisted of empty threats and half-baked ideas. Unlike the outcome of meetings in the past, this one would end in no satisfactory resolution for the good people of Silverville. Their adversaries were too powerful.

She checked her watch. Nothing to be gained at the meeting. Time for her to carry out the plan. Clutching her purse and sweater, Lela made her way to the door as unobtrusively as possible.

Grady and Leona must have come to the same conclusion and ducked out early, too. They walked together toward the parking lot, Grady insisting they escort her to her car. When they arrived, Lela faced Grady.

"Perry said you'd taken a Day Trip by accident."

The rancher frowned. "Somethin' happened. Not sure what. I was thinking about my great-great grand pappy back in his day, and suddenly I *was* him. Darnedest dream I ever had."

Perry had told Lela Day Trippers landed in random bodies, but Grady was telling her he'd landed in the body of the specific person he'd thought about. Did the Ka Catchers know that? According to her husband, they'd yet to discover completely how it all worked. If someone could dictate who they wanted to be, it could make a journey into the past a lot more predictable – not the way Buford's misadventure as a little kid turned out.

She thanked Grady and hugged Leona good-bye. Getting in her car, she thought again about the old rancher's final words. She'd carry out the plan, but not exactly the way Perry suggested.

THE SHOPPING cart rattled with every pebble it hit, and one of the wheels squeaked with each rotation. The darn thing had barely fit in the back of her compact SUV, now parked a couple hundred yards from the Ka Catcher entrance. Lela fought the urge to pull up the nylons riding around her ankles – the perfect accessory to the tattered skirt and combat boots she'd worn at last fall's Halloween party. In her opinion, the outfit made for a pretty hot bag lady.

With each lurch of the basket, Breakfast squealed with mournful complaints. Lela paused to pat her. *Has to be better riding in a basket than a windshield.* Leading her with a leash was out of the question; she moved too slowly. Almost as slow as the Prince of Yadim, who trailed behind her at the end of a rope. Every now and then the slack in the tether stretched taut, and she had to tug him along.

"You're walking too fast for him," Howard spoke in hushed tones. "Don't think he sees too well in the dark."

"You don't have to whisper, Howard. They can't help but hear us coming." The sound effects worked perfectly. She wanted the guards to hear.

Steering the cart off the road and down the driveway, she saw the frozen silhouettes of two figures backlit by the floodlights of the compound. They'd probably never seen a bag lady pushing a pig in a shopping cart and leading a man by a leash.

Lela's little entourage squeaked, rattled, and squealed their way up to the closed gate beside the guard house, the soldiers on duty apparently too stunned by the sight to stop their approach.

She slowed the cart and fished a corncob pipe out of her skirt pocket. "Got a light?"

The nearest man stared open-mouthed for a few seconds before he ordered, "Keep moving! You don't have any business here."

"I think I do." She pulled Mr. Smith into the light and removed the leash. "Does this man look familiar?"

Lela sure hoped he did because she and Howard had spent an hour earlier that afternoon holding him down and dyeing his hair back to black. She couldn't take credit for this part of the plan. Perry came up with the idea to return the prince to create a diversion while she sneaked into the outhouse. She'd seen the photos of the prince on TV, a dandy in a blazer covered with braids and medals and wearing a beret. The thrift shop didn't carry anything like that, so she settled on an old black and red Star Trek uniform.

The guards stepped closer and shined a flashlight through the chain-link gate to take a look. They exchanged glances and shrugged.

"No," they said in unison.

Perry had assured her they'd recognize him right away. The finishing touch was the prince's flashy jewelry April had hidden in her apartment, which Lela retrieved and placed on his wrist and fingers. "Gotta be the same man who's been all over the news. The missing prince?"

They returned blank stares.

So much for subtlety. She'd have to spell it out for these guards. "C'mon, you two. You must know who I mean. The Prince of Yadim." Lela pointed to the Rolex and diamond rings. "Who else would wear jewelry like that? Better get somebody else out here."

The taller guard nodded to his companion, who began trotting back toward the Welcome Center.

The next few minutes would determine whether or not she could pull this off. Perry had suggested that Howard would create the diversion by revealing Mr. Smith. In all the confusion sure to follow, she was to slip away and enter the outhouse. When Perry explained his plan, *she* seemed the logical choice since the person returning to the past would land in a random body. That kind of complication required fast thinking and resourcefulness. But after talking to Grady and finding out the time-traveler could dictate the identity, it changed everything. The diversion could be the messier part; almost anyone could return to burn down the outhouse. Hopefully, even Howard.

She'd coached him before they got to Ka Catchers to concentrate on thinking about himself, Silverville, and six months ago once he went inside The Time Portal. Landing in his own body, all he had to do was find some gasoline and a match, and no one would find his behavior any stranger than usual.

But first, they had to get past the gate and nearer the outhouse.

Within minutes, the soldier returned alongside three men wearing suits. April's *Men in Black*, she assumed.

"What's this all about?" demanded one who wore brown rather than black.

So much for stereotypes. At least Lela could get back on script. "This guy claims he's the Prince of Yadim."

"Open the gate," said the Man in Brown.

The soldiers hopped at his quiet command, rolling the fence open. At the same time, Lela pushed the cart and Breakfast inside as Howard led the prince.

All flashlights aimed at the man wearing the Star Trek uniform, scanning him up and down. He stood as motionless as a giant unblinking turnip.

Mr. Man in Brown waved his hand in front of the human vegetable. No response.

'He comes and goes," Lela offered. "Right now, mostly gone. Thought at first he was stoned. But every now and then he's alert," she lied.

She edged the cart a little deeper into the compound as she continued to talk. "He told me he was the Prince of Yadim, and he kinda looks like him, from the pictures on TV, dontcha think?" She motioned Howard to follow as she ventured further inside. "When he was lucid for a few minutes, he talked about this place. So I decided to bring him here. Closer for me than Yadim."

One of the other MIB asked, "How'd you wind up with this man?"

Lela expected that question. Grinning, she answered, "Found him while making my rounds to the dumpsters. He tried to take my watermelon rinds away from me. 'No way,' I told him. 'Rinds make good pickles,' I said."

Lela pretended to rummage in her skirt pockets. "Wanna try one?"

The men backed away, shaking their heads no.

"Anywho, after that he followed me home. Thought he might make a good butler. Terrible at it, though."

"We need some sort of identification. Do you have a driver's license?" Mr. Brown Suit asked.

Lela let out a cackle. "If I did, you think I'd be pushing this cart around?"

The Man in Brown ordered the tall guard to help his colleagues escort the alleged prince inside. To the short guard, he said, "Get these other people and the pig off the premises."

Then he strode after the MIB delegation surrounding the prince. Exactly what Lela had hoped would happen. Now she only had to deal with one guard instead of two.

The remaining soldier placed a hand on her shoulder and started to nudge her in the direction of the gate. "Move along now."

Lela dipped out of his reach and turned toward him. "Wait, wait! First we have to sing happy birthday to you."

He started laughing. "My birthday isn't for six more weeks."

"We'll sing it early then." She circled behind the shopping cart, maneuvering the man to face her, with his back to the outhouse. Using her corncob pipe as a maestro's baton, she said, "Hit it, Breakfast. Happy birthday to you …"

The pig let loose with a cacophony of grunts and squeals that almost matched her tempo. The floodlights lit the side of the guard's face, which looked on in disbelief.

Right on cue, Howard began to edge away. *Good boy.*

"Happy birthday to youuuuu …"

More grunts and squeals.

The guard politely waited for her and Breakfast to finish their song, but Howard had made it only two-thirds the way to his destination.

"Thanks. Very nice, lady," the soldier said, appearing to humor her. "Now keep moving."

"But that's not all." She pulled a smashed cupcake from one pocket and sparkler from the other. "You gotta have a birthday cake."

Lela poked the sparkler into the cupcake and reached back into her pocket. "Oh, here's my lighter."

Igniting the "candle," she offered it to the guard.

He jumped back to avoid getting burned by the sparks. "What the hell?"

He stood mesmerized, like a little kid on the Fourth of July. Enough time for Lela's co-conspirator to make it to the outhouse.

When the candle fizzled out, the guard looked past her. "Hey! Where's that other guy?"

She smiled. Now it was up to Howard.

HOWARD Beacon, six months ago, Silverville. Howard Beacon, six months ago, Silverville. He repeated the words, like Lela coached him. Closing the door to the little outhouse, the first thing he noticed was the stink. The second thing he noticed was the embalming table.

"Howard? Howard!" Mr. Fine spoke louder than usual. His boss stood on the other side of the table. In between them lay Mr. Slattery.

Oh yeah, I remember this. Mr. Slattery died six months ago. Wow, I must have time-traveled. The next day, the deceased's wife would get super mad when she saw his toupee on backwards. Howard had stuck it on his head the wrong way, but to him both sides looked the same. Tomorrow he'd be more careful and ask Mr. Fine which way it went.

"When you're done daydreaming, hand me the Superglue," Mr. Fine said.

Howard handed it to him from the stand nearby, and the mortician squeezed a little bead along Mr. Slattery's lower lip, pressing and holding the two lips together.

"I've got to go," Howard said.

"You know where the bathroom is."

"No, I mean, I've got to do something."

Mr. Fine looked up from the lips. "At eleven at night?"

Howard panicked. Lela had told him not to tell anybody what he was going to do. He scrunched up his mouth, thinking for a full two minutes. What could he say? "I have to feed my goldfish."

"You don't have any goldfish."

"Oh, that's right."

They finished the embalming, and the two of them moved the body to a gurney and rolled it next door. Mr. Fine always went up front to do the paperwork while Howard cleaned the prep room. He'd have to clean fast. Scrubbing down the table, he thought about the instructions Lela had given. *Find some gas, get a lighter, go to the outhouse, burn it down.*

He hoped he could remember everything.

After he wiped down the table, he mopped the floor and put all the instruments back in the cabinet. He picked up the dirty towels and sheets, dropping them into a hamper. Almost done. He took one more look around to make sure everything was just like Mr. Fine wanted. A spool of surgical thread still sat on top of the embalming machine. Uh-oh. It was so hard to do his job right while remembering to *find some gas, get a lighter, go to the outhouse, burn it down.* Returning the thread to the cabinet, he flipped off the lights and went up front.

"I'm all done, Mr. Fine."

His boss didn't even look up from the desk. "Good job. See you tomorrow."

Howard walked back down the hall to the garage, put on his helmet, and got on his bike. The Short Stop convenience store might still be open. Everything seemed so dark as he pedaled down the street. Then he realized his headlight had burned out when it was six months ago. Good thing he didn't see any cars on the road. Each time his foot pressed down, he repeated Lela's words in his head.

Once he arrived at the Short Stop, the store's lights were still on. He put his kickstand down and went inside.

"Evenin', Howard," the clerk said. "What you doing out so late?"

"Gotta get some gas, get a lighter, and go – well, do some other stuff."

The clerked laughed. "Sounds like you're gonna burn something down."

Howard panicked again. But the man didn't give him a chance to say anything else. The clerk walked to an aisle and picked up a gas can and returned to the checkout counter. He reached over to a display and pulled off a lighter. "Zippo okay?"

Howard nodded.

The clerked punched buttons on the register, saying, "Okay, one can, one Zippo, one gallon of gas. That'll be $14.29."

Digging into his pocket, Howard found a ten-dollar bill and a pop bottle cap. He put both on the counter. "All I got is this."

"Tell ya what, I'll spot you the rest. Come by tomorrow and pay me the difference."

Howard thanked him and went outside to pump gas. Screwing on the cap, he placed the gas can in the bicycle basket and steered his bike onto the street. He knew the way to Ka Catchers even in the dark, and his own cabin was only a couple miles past that. All the pedaling sure made him hungry. When he got home, he'd heat up a can of chili. Maybe with Ritz crackers and dill pickles. First, he'd line the bottom of the bowl with sliced pickles and top them with crumbled crackers. But not too thick. Pickles tended to get soggy if they waited too long on the bottom of the bowl.

The road in front of his bike lit up and he heard a siren chirp behind him. Nearly losing his balance, he wobbled to the side of the road and looked over his shoulder. It was Sheriff Carl, who pulled up alongside him and rolled down his passenger window.

"Whatcha doing out so late, Howard?"

"Riding my bike."

The sheriff grinned. "I can see that. But do you know you don't have any lights?"

"I know. I'll get new ones when they go on sale at the hardware store."

"Be sure to do that. And don't ride this bike at night 'til you get them replaced."

"Yes, sir."

The sheriff switched on and shined his spotlight at Howard's basket. "What's with the gas?"

For the third time that night, Howard panicked. What if Sheriff Carl had guessed what he was gonna do?

"Planning to mow your lawn?" the sheriff asked.

"I don't have a lawn."

The sheriff laughed. "Wish I didn't either. Well, take care getting home." He rolled up his window and drove away.

Howard sighed with relief. He got back on the bike and pedaled toward Ka Catchers. He was almost there. Got the gas, got the lighter. Now just burn down the outhouse. He could do this, and Lela would be proud of him.

The road was so dark he nearly missed the turn-in. Veering sharp, he bounced up the rut leading into the driveway. He could see the Welcome Center ahead as the moon peeked over S Hill. Didn't look like the place he remembered. Just an old ranch house. While he stared at the building, his tire hit something in the gravel, flipping him and the bike to the ground. He picked himself up and limped to the bicycle.

The basket was empty.

Oh, no! He felt in his pocket; the Zippo was still there. But the gas can had disappeared. He ran in circles around the bike until he tripped on a heavy object, which sloshed and tumbled end over end into sagebrush by the side of the driveway. The gas can! He picked it up and heard a dribble. The smell of gasoline filled the air. His fall must've punctured the can.

Howard ran fast as he could toward the outhouse before all the gas leaked out. With each step, the can felt a little lighter. When he reached the little building, he unscrewed the cap and splashed what was left of the gas on the front. It wasn't much. Flipping open the Zippo, he raked his thumb over the tiny wheel until it created a flame. He touched it to the door, and a small flicker of fire burned up the drops of gas staining the wood. Within seconds, the flame died.

Several more times, he flicked the lighter on and pushed it against the door. Nothing.

He stepped back, the Zippo still burning, and used the flame to watch for any sign of smoke.

"Ouch!" His hand dropped the hot lighter.

Poof! A line of fire raced away from the outhouse, following the dribbled trail of gasoline. Howard ran behind it and stomped at the flames, but the soles of his shoes got too hot. By the time he jumped out of the way, the sage beside the driveway began to blaze and spread. He watched the fire work its way toward the ranch house. Within minutes, it too went up in flames.

He didn't mean for this to happen, and he didn't think Lela would be happy. The fire roared, leaping from the house to the garage to the barn, catching dry grass and consuming more and more ground.

Hopping over hot embers, he ran to the driveway and picked up his bike. Just before he pedaled away, he looked back at the roaring flames.

To his horror, the only thing not ablaze was the outhouse, standing in a perfect little island of untouched grass.

epilogue

April pushed a book cart down the aisle in the Silverville Public Library. She'd only had the intern job for a couple of weeks, but already she felt in control. Mrs. Brumbelow had taken to walking away whenever April started one of the tales about her past. Suited her, the old bat didn't have much imagination.

An older man with thick white hair blocked the aisle, sitting on the floor surrounded by a pile of books.

"Can I help you?" she asked.

He looked up, his eyes fixing on her contact lenses. Today, she'd worn a pair of her favorites, half moons in honor of the summer equinox.

"Looking at these?" she asked, pointing to her lenses. "Fun designer stuff."

He smiled and nodded. "Actually, you can help me find something. I need a book on hauntings. My wife Lela thought she saw a ghost the other night. Of all things, a cowboy ghost. I told her I'd research it."

"Huh, that's interesting. I heard there're some haunted buildings here in town. Have you thought about getting an EVP recorder?"

"What's that?"

"Electronic voice phenomena. My folks are famous international ghost hunters. They use EVPs all the time."

"Sounds like a great job. Ya know, I've been pretty bored since I retired, and I'm looking to find some sort of new adventure. Maybe I'll invest in one of those EVPs, give it a shot. And we can invite you over to give me and Lela some tips."

"I can do that. I'll be here all summer." She backed out of the aisle and detoured around the computer carousel.

That same boy she'd seen all week sat hunched over one of the screens. Typical computer geek, which she usually avoided. Still, there was something about him that had captured her attention, and she was sure she'd caught him looking at her.

She maneuvered the book cart to bump into his chair. "Sorry. Anything I can help you with?"

He looked up and stared at her lenses, rolled his eyes. Then he went back to his computer.

She leaned over his shoulder to study the screen. "Alchemy? Turning lead into gold?"

"Well, yeah. That and other stuff."

"When I was a kid living in South America, my parents knew a shaman who dabbled in alchemy, mostly for the metaphysics."

That got his attention.

"I'll try to remember the stuff he taught us. Wanna talk about it over coffee sometime?"

BUFORD spread architectural drawings across the hood of his car. No surprise the construction company was behind schedule.

The past three months had been a real roller-coaster. First he'd found the perfect location for the shooting range, something he'd long wanted to build to complement his business in town.

230

Second, he bought the winning lottery ticket. Two and a half million. Things looked like they were going his way.

Until Howard came over with his damn pet pig. He was about to leave the house and cash in his ticket, but that idiot just had to show him how the animal could sing "Happy Birthday." Buford had the ticket in hand, watching Howard's carrot baton. It only took a flash. The pig snatched the ticket from his fingers and swallowed it. Buford thrust his hand into the pig's throat, managing to recover half.

"Well, you can wait 'til the other half comes out later," Howard had said.

The numbers on the retrieved half had already begun to dissolve. Potent pig saliva.

"Get that beast out of here, or I'll eat it for breakfast!"

Took him a long time to get over that. He sure could have used the money for the gun range improvements. It was bad luck and bacon lost.

Buford heard a vehicle coming up the driveway. Carl eased his squad car to a halt and got out.

"Man, this place sure looks different since Howard burned it down," the sheriff said.

"Yeah, saved me a lot of trouble. I'd planned to have it all bulldozed anyway."

Carl leaned against the hood. "Damnedest thing. When I talked to him the next morning, he couldn't remember any of it."

"Or didn't want to remember. He should've been arrested."

"Naw, he was telling the truth. Just an accident. Dark road, gas can spark. Could've happened to anyone. All this dried up wood was just waiting for an excuse."

Buford folded up his architectural plans and pointed to a new cement foundation. "In a few weeks, the clubhouse is gonna be where the old ranch house stood." He swiveled around and swept his arms toward the rest of the property. "And that area back where the outhouse stood will be the shooting range."

Carl cupped his eyes and scanned the flattened ground beyond the new foundation. "What happened to that old outhouse? Seems I recall it was the only thing left standing after the fire."

"Yep, it was. I came out that next morning to take a look. Don't know why it didn't burn."

"Outhouses are full of moisture, old mold. Must have been what saved it."

Buford stuffed the plans into his briefcase. "Anyway, I had the dozers cover it up."

Carl started for his car. "Probably good thing you flattened it."

"Yeah, if I left it standing, might be a problem in the future."

THE END

ABOUT THE AUTHORS

Kym O'Connell-Todd is a writer and graphic designer. **Mark Todd** is a college professor and program director for Western State Colorado University's MFA in Creative Writing. They live in the Cochetopa Mountains east of Gunnison with more animals than most reasonable people would feed.

Kym and Mark with the real "Breakfast," who can sing "Happy Birthday." Go to http://youtu.be/9nTSzqDTXBU to hear her rendition.1

Visit the authors' website:

www.writeinthethick.com

IF YOU ENJOYED "THE MAGICKE OUTHOUSE" WE'RE SURE YOU'LL LIKE THE OTHER
TWO BOOKS IN THE SILVERVILLE SAGA

Little Greed Men (Book One)

All Plucked Up (Book Two)

For more information visit

www.raspberrycreekbooks.com

CPSIA information can be obtained
at www.ICGtesting.com
Printed in the USA
FFOW02n1131131113
2342FF